Kaleidoscope

By Dorothy Gilman

PUBLISHED BY THE BALLANTINE PUBLISHING GROUP

CARAVAN

UNCERTAIN VOYAGE

A NUN IN THE CLOSET

THE CLAIRVOYANT COUNTESS

THE TIGHTROPE WALKER

INCIDENT AT BADAMYÂ

THALE'S FOLLY

The Mrs. Pollifax Series

THE UNEXPECTED MRS. POLLIFAX

THE AMAZING MRS. POLLIFAX

THE ELUSIVE MRS. POLLIFAX

A PALM FOR MRS. POLLIFAX

MRS. POLLIFAX ON SAFARI

MRS. POLLIFAX ON THE CHINA STATION

MRS. POLLIFAX AND THE HONG KONG BUDDHA

MRS. POLLIFAX AND THE GOLDEN TRIANGLE

MRS. POLLIFAX AND THE WHIRLING DERVISH

MRS. POLLIFAX AND THE SECOND THIEF

MRS. POLLIFAX PURSUED

MRS. POLLIFAX AND THE LION KILLER

MRS. POLLIFAX, INNOCENT TOURIST

MRS. POLLIFAX UNVEILED

For Young Adults

GIRL IN BUCKSKIN

THE MAZE IN THE HEART OF THE CASTLE

THE BELLS OF FREEDOM

Nonfiction

A NEW KIND OF COUNTRY

Kaleidoscope

a Countess Karitska novel

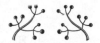

Dorothy Gilman

BALLANTINE BOOKS • NEW YORK

To Chris, Beth, John, and Jackie

psychometry: the divination of facts concerning an object or its owner through contact with or to the object

clairvoyance: the ability to perceive matter beyond the range of ordinary perception
—*Webster's New Collegiate Dictionary,* 1963–1973

1

Madame Karitska, leaving the shabby brownstone on Eighth Street, gave only a cursory glance at the sign in the first-floor window that read MADAME KARITSKA, READINGS. It was ironic, she thought as she stepped into the bright noon sunshine, how a talent that had earned her whippings as a child, and for which she had never before accepted money, had led her so firmly to this street a year ago, and to this brownstone, to place the sign in the window that at last admitted her gift of clairvoyance.

On the other hand, her life had always been filled with surprises, and among them, here in Trafton, was her blossoming friendship with Detective Lieutenant Pruden, whose suspicions and skepticism had long since been obliterated by the help she'd been able to offer him in his work. The shoddiness of the neighborhood neither bothered nor depressed her; after all, she had known poverty in Kabul, and wealth in Antwerp, and poverty again in America, and in spite of Eighth Street's flirting with decay it no longer seemed to deter her clients, which amused her. She was becoming known.

At the moment, however, she was between appointments

and free to venture uptown for a few purchases, and she was in no hurry; she walked slowly, drinking in the sounds and colors along the way as if they were intoxicating, as for her they were. Reaching Tenth Street she saw that the warmth of the sun had brought Sreja Zagredi out of his secondhand furniture store to sit in the sun, and she greeted him cordially.

His eyes brightened. "Ah, Madame Karitska, you have the step of a young girl!"

"And you the heart of a brigand," she told him. "How is my rug today?"

"Still here," he told her, pointing to it displayed in the window. "I have a very good offer for it the other day, from a man uptown who appreciates the finest of old rugs, I assure you."

"Nonsense," said Madame Karitska crisply, "it's a poor copy of an Oriental rug, and shabby as well."

"Shabby! A good rug ages like wine," he told her indignantly. "You want garish colors, God forbid? A hundred dollars is still my price, but only for you."

Madame Karitska smiled. "The colors *were* garish," she pointed out amiably, "but you've had it hanging in the sun all winter, spring and summer to fade it. My offer remains eighty-five dollars."

"Eighty-five!" He pulled at his considerable hair in anguish. "What a fool you make of me to tell this stranger from uptown I save it for a friend! With five children to feed you speak starvation to me, Madame Karitska."

She observed him critically. "Scarcely starving. I think you could lose at least twenty pounds, Mr. Zagredi, if you cut down on the *brînză* and the raki."

"This is a rug worth at least one hundred fifty uptown!"

Madame Karitska shrugged. "Then take it uptown, Mr. Zagredi."

He blew through his mustache and eyed her shrewdly. "For you I have already come down to one hundred."

"And for you I have already gone up to eighty-five," she reminded him.

They eyed each other appreciatively, and he laughed. "There is no one like you anymore, Madame Karitska; you know how to haggle like in the old country and it does my heart good. Like the knife—sharp!"

"Very sharp, yes," she told him cheerfully. "In the meantime it is good to see you, and say hello to your wife for me, Mr. Zagredi."

"Come for a dinner of *mămăligă*," he called after her. "Come soon—you are the only one who can put sense into my son's head about school."

"I will," she promised, smiling, and they parted with perfect understanding, their minds pleasantly exercised and soothed by the exchange.

Reaching the subway station at Eleventh Street she paid her fare and was pleased to find a seat available. In the moment before the doors slammed shut, two men entered the car, one of them young, with a hard, suntanned face that almost matched the color of his trench coat, and who took a seat some distance away. The other, older man wore a dark, somewhat shabby suit and carried a small attaché case, and he sat down opposite her; glancing at him she gave a start, for she recognized him. Leaning forward she was about to call across the aisle to him when he lifted his head and looked directly at her and then through her, with not a trace of expression on his face.

At once Madame Karitska covered her movement by leaning down and retying a shoelace. When she straightened again she studied the man briefly and glanced away, but she was alert now, and thoughtful.

The train stopped at the next station and the man opposite her half rose, as if to leave, and then sank back. When he did this Madame Karitska noticed that farther down the car the man in the trench coat also made a move to leave and then aborted it. Seeing this she returned her glance to the impassive face across the aisle, and this time he met her gaze, and without expression they gazed at each other for a long moment.

At Fifteenth Street her friend in the shabby suit stood up, carrying his attaché case, and walked to the door to stand beside it as the train swayed to a halt. He was followed by the young man in the trench coat, but Madame Karitska saw him adroitly step aside to allow a woman to precede him, which placed him next to the younger man instead of in front of him. The doors slid open; the man with the attaché case walked out, hesitated and then stopped, allowing others to swarm past him.

Just as the doors began to close behind him he turned, looked back at Madame Karitska, and lifting his arm he threw his attaché case to her; she caught it in her lap just as the doors slammed shut. The last she saw of its owner he was hurrying toward the stairs to the street while the man in the trench coat stared back into the car, mouth slightly open, his eyes fixed on Madame Karitska. As the train picked up speed he turned and ran after the older man.

No one in the subway car appeared startled that Madame Karitska had been tossed a small attaché case by an apparent stranger. At the next station she left the train, and once above ground she signaled a cruising taxi: this was one time, she felt, when it was expedient not to be walking the streets, for unless Georges Verlag had changed his occupation since she had known him in Europe, he had just tossed her an attaché case filled with diamonds.

Ten minutes later she regained her apartment and drew a sigh of relief. Placing the attaché case on her square coffee table she examined its several locks and nodded, reasonably sure now that Georges was still a diamond salesman, and that the case contained a delivery of jewels worth a hundred thousand dollars, if not more. Georges had always been one of the best, as well as a good friend of her late husband, who had been a diamond merchant, and they had frequently entertained Georges in their Antwerp home. It had been a long time ago, but since she herself was now in America was it really so surprising that Georges, too, was here?

She thought a moment and then went to the phone and dialed police headquarters, asking for Lieutenant Pruden.

"He's out," said the desk sergeant. "Is this Madame Karitska?"

"Ah, Margolies," she said, "what a good ear you have for

voices. Yes, would you ask him to call me, please, when he returns? It's quite important."

"Righto," said Margolies. "Your ESP working again? He's out on a hit-and-run case, but— Hold on, he's just walked in."

A second later Pruden was greeting her warmly.

"Something has happened," she said calmly, "so that I wonder if you could stop in here today at your convenience. I would have gone directly to the precinct if I could have been sure you were in, but—"

"That bad?" he said lightly. "Actually I can come right now, I'm leaving in a minute and will be passing your street. Serious?" he added in a lower voice.

"Not precisely a criminal matter—not yet," she explained.

"Be there in five minutes," he said, and hung up.

In precisely five minutes a police car drew up to her building and Pruden was at her door. Entering her apartment he gave a quick glance around the room and then a look at her face as she brought out the tray of Turkish coffee and placed it on the table. "Thank you for stopping, this won't take long," she told him.

His level brows lifted over his slate gray eyes. "I thought at the very least you were being held captive here. Margolies said it was important?"

She nodded. "I think so," and pouring out the lavalike brew she handed him a cup and began describing to him her experience on the subway train. "You see," she explained, "when Georges first moved to go—and then didn't—he was very definitely showing me that he was being followed. When he did leave at the next stop"—from beneath the table she drew out the attaché case and handed it to Pruden—"he threw this to me just as the doors closed behind him."

He looked at it, frowning. "Nothing too unusual about it. You say you recognized this man?"

"His name is Georges Verlag," she told him, "and I believe you will find at least a hundred thousand dollars' worth of diamonds in this case."

His brows shot skyward again.

"No, I'm not being clairvoyant now," she said, smiling. "Georges I knew in Europe. You may recall that I was married once to a diamond merchant in Antwerp. Georges was a young diamond salesman then, and I have few doubts that he still is. This is how diamonds are often carried for delivery."

"This casually?"

"Oh yes," she said, "but you mustn't think there is anything casual about their travel arrangements. Diamond salesmen have to be very clever and very, very cautious, never staying at the same hotel twice, often making a reservation at one place and then going to another, never announcing where or when or how. They would equal in deception any CIA agents."

"I've never known either," Pruden said, his eyes on the case. "I do see that it has three locks and is made of steel. You realize that if these are diamonds, then your friend placed you in some danger by tossing the case to you?"

"The danger is negligible," she told him with a shrug. "How could that man in the trench coat learn who I am?"

Pruden said dryly, "By catching up with your friend Verlag and insisting, not too gently, that he identify you."

She nodded, smiling. "I did hope that might not occur to you. There is, however, no certainty that Georges knows my present name, since it was Von Domm at that period in my life."

Pruden grinned at her. "If I've finally gotten it all straight I am speaking to—let's see—the Countess Marina Elena Provotchnichet Gaylord Von Domm Karitska?"

"You say it very musically," she told him.

"But I still don't like any of this. Who does Verlag work for, do you know?"

She shook her head. "I've no idea, but there used to be only two very large dealers in this country: Winston and the Zale Corporation. And I should like you please to take them away with you and place them somewhere very safe."

He nodded. "Of course, but we'll have to open the case to verify its contents, you know. The chief wouldn't care to tuck away an attaché case full of hashish or cocaine. Look, you're sure about this? Your friend Verlag could be on your doorstep in an hour or two wanting this back, you know."

"I would be most happy if Georges does appear on my doorstep inside of the hour," she told him, "for I am more than a little worried about him; I did not at all like the look of the man following him. But if Georges should arrive, he will have to visit headquarters for his case, for I refuse to keep anything of value on Eighth Street."

Pruden nodded and put down his cup of coffee. "I'll leave

you with a receipt for one leather-covered steel attaché case with three locks and a scar on one corner, presumably the property of one Georges Verlag, and in turn you'll let me know the minute you hear from him."

"Agreed," she told him.

With a glance at his watch he nodded. "I'll just have time to drop this off at the station, I'm due to interview the parents of a young girl killed by a hit-and-run driver over in Ardsley, her funeral only three days ago."

"So young! Poor child!"

He turned at the door to give her a thoughtful glance. "Poor child, yes, but something . . ." He frowned.

"Yes?"

"Something about it troubles me and I don't know what. Do you suppose . . ." He reached into his pocket. "I'm to deliver this gold cross to her parents, found by the Ardsley police on the street, after—well, it was there when the ambulance came. They've washed the blood from it. Do you suppose you'd have time to . . . to . . . I could return it to them tomorrow or by mail."

"Of course," she told him. "There'll be time for that after my next appointment—to see what impressions I can receive?"

He placed the gold cross with its torn thread of a necklace on her table. "Thanks," he said, and hurried out, leaving Madame Karitska to turn her attention to devising a message for Georges Verlag, and with haste, since her two o'clock appointment loomed.

With a pen she scribbled a few lines on paper, crossed them out, and then clarified them until she had reached a message too oblique to enlighten anyone but Georges—if, of course, he read the newspaper personals: G, she wrote, and in block letters, *IN MEMORY OF ANTWERP TRY KARITSKA, NOT M. VON D.*" She then phoned the classified section of the newspaper and asked that it be inserted in tomorrow's edition, and for three more days, and after writing out a check she mailed this at the corner postbox. When this had been done she cleared the coffee table of cups and carried them into her tiny kitchen, where a *tajine* was simmering on the stove. She had time only to stir it when her two o'clock appointment knocked at the door. She opened it to a young woman with an anxious face, who simply stared at her, apparently not expecting a tall, distinguished-looking woman with oddly hooded eyes and a kind smile.

The girl promptly burst into tears.

"Oh my dear, you are much too young to cry," said Madame Karitska gently. "Do come inside." For her, she decided, a cup of rich cocoa with a fillip of whipped cream. "You shall have some hot chocolate, which will make you feel better," and drawing her inside she returned to her kitchen. When she entered the living room again, tray in hand, the girl was seated on the couch, staring at the wall of books, at the intricately carved Chinese coffee table, and at the sun streaming through the window.

She blurted out, "My name's Betsy Oliver," and then— again startled—she added, "I didn't expect you to look so . . . so . . . I thought you'd look more like a gypsy fortune-teller."

"Life is full of disappointments, is it not," said Madame
Karitska humorously, and leaning across the table handed her
the cup of steaming cocoa. "You are feeling better now?"

The girl nodded, and Madame Karitska gave her a brief but
thorough glance, noting the anxiety in her eyes and the air of
helplessness she projected. But although the helplessness
might be real to her, thought Madame Karitska, it was either
self-imposed or imposed by others, for she was *not* the little
brown wren that she believed herself, dressed as she was in
colorless clothes. Her face was too strong, and her jaw too firm.

"It's my husband," Betsy Oliver said, and reaching into her
purse she brought out a large signet ring. "Mona told me you
hold things—"

"Psychometry, yes," said Madame Karitska.

"Mona's the friend who recommended you. So I brought
Alpha's ring. My husband's. He thinks he mislaid it, but . . ."
She flushed. "I'll tell him tonight I found it behind the sofa
cushions or somewhere."

"An interesting name, Alpha," said Madame Karitska.

"Well, actually it's Arthur," the girl said with a vague mo-
tion of her hand. "We've been married seven years, but
lately—well, he's joined this group a year ago and they gave
him that name, you see. I guess he likes it, so he's kept it."

"Alpha," mused Madame Karitska. "A religious group?"

She looked uncertain. "It must be; he brings home all
these pamphlets about righteousness and not wearing jewelry, and the meek inheriting the earth, and the evils of—
And I have to braid my hair, not let it hang loose."

"Perhaps a cult?" suggested Madame Karitska.

Tears came again to the girl's eyes. "Whatever it is I can't understand how it changed him. We can't go to the movies anymore, or play card games, and he used to love playing cards and movies."

"Does the group have a name?"

She nodded. "Guardians of Eden. They have a big place out in the Edgerton section—an estate, he says—and *now* . . . now he wants us to go—all of us, me and our daughter, she's five—wants us to go there to *live*." Tears were running down her cheeks now. "He's out almost every night and—" She burst into tears. "I'm scared."

"Yes," said Madame Karitska. "Yes, you would be. May I have something of yours to hold?"

"Mine! But it's Arthur—I mean Alpha—I hoped you could explain."

"In a moment, yes," she assured her. "But it helps me to know you as well."

With some effort the girl removed the ring on her left hand with its tiny diamond, then brought out a handkerchief and blew her nose.

Closing her eyes Madame Karitska stilled her mind and opened herself to the vibrations and feelings that the ring had accumulated from its years of being worn. She rejected the negatives one by one—the emanations of dreariness and monotony and routine—and was surprised and pleased to reach below these to something so promising. "I wonder," she said, opening her eyes, "if you realize you have a very real talent in art. Do you sketch? Paint?"

The girl turned scarlet. "Oh, Alpha doesn't allow—" She

stopped, flustered yet looking pleased. "Do you really think I have *talent* for it?"

Madame Karitska nodded. "You do sketch, then."

Looking frightened, and then defiant, the girl brought from her purse a small sheet of paper. "I burn them usually but I can't stop, it's what keeps me going. It doesn't look like much," she said, and handed it across the table.

Madame Karitska looked at it, and to her surprise tears rose in her eyes. It was a simple line drawing of a child's face, very free, very spontaneous and fresh, the nose, brows, and lips only suggested, the eyes luminous and wondering. "Oh my dear," she said, deeply touched.

The girl looked at her in surprise. "You think it's good?"

"Exquisite. You have the gift of rejecting the unimportant and seeing the essence, a gift that comes naturally to only the best. And the way the lines flow . . ." She smiled at the girl. "I'm delighted to have met you."

"You really think—But Alpha . . ."

She was not ready for it, of course, realized Madame Karitska; her attention was concentrated totally on her husband, it had been demanded of her, and she was not accustomed to thinking of herself. Madame Karitska handed back the ring and picked up Arthur's—or Alpha's, as he preferred to be called now, and she sighed a little, wondering how women could so rashly turn their selves over to such unpromising men. There was really nothing unpleasant about Alpha, she found, her eyes closed, but she received no sense of real character or stability, a man loosely held together by rules, compulsion, the needs of wife and children, ambitious but lacking the discipline to fulfill those ambitions: a dreamer . . . some charm, of course, but weak. He so obviously dominated his wife that she would be shocked to learn how malleable he really was.

She opened her eyes, very serious now. "I can tell you very little of what you want to know, except that I feel very strongly that you face a very, very difficult decision."

"What?" the girl asked despairingly.

"Your husband, I feel . . ." She hesitated and then, "No, I must be blunt. I feel that you will lose your husband whether you go with him to this Guardian of Eden home or not. I don't mean to be melodramatic—perhaps you cannot even understand it, or why—but he has already given himself over to them. His sense of self, perhaps even his soul."

"You mean . . . he'll insist our little girl and I must go?"

"I feel that you will have to choose," Madame Karitska said gently. "Choose between the Guardians of Eden and your husband. You will need all your strength."

The girl stared at her helplessly. "But I have no strength, not without *him*."

"If you think that, then of course you must join him—but I do not think you realize what strength you have, or what talent. But the answer has to come from yourself—inside—not from others." She rose from her chair and placed both hands on the girl's shoulders. "Think," she told her. "Think and feel. I'm sorry to have upset you, but I have, frankly, feelings not very good about this group of your husband's." *Or your husband either*, she thought, but did not say.

DOROTHY GILMAN   15

Betsy nodded. "That's what I didn't *want* to hear, isn't it."
She sighed and stood up, looking miserable. "What do you
charge?" she asked, opening her purse.

Madame Karitska had a vision of the wallet, very thin and
worn, with its few dollars, its grocery lists. She said, "I would
prefer—would love to have that little sketch of the child—
your daughter, isn't it? If you could spare that, it would be far
more meaningful to me than any money."

"Spare it!" she said joyously. "But how wonderful, I'd only
be throwing it away."

"*Don't,*" said Madame Karitska with passion. "*Don't* de-
stroy your work, do *more* of it. Sketch everything that pleases
you, whenever you have a free moment. Hide your work if you
must, but never, *never* throw it away."

The girl looked at her, torn by doubt. "It's very small in
size," she said, handing it to her.

"I will frame and hang it and I shall cherish it," Madame
Karitska told the girl warmly. "Come back and see it framed
in a week or two if you'd like."

She nodded. "Yes—*yes,*" she said eagerly, "I will. And
thank you." And then, startled, she asked, "Why do you suddenly look like that?"

Because, thought Madame Karitska sadly, *there is no happiness for you ahead—not yet, not yet,* and she opened the
door for her. "Take care, my dear," she told her, and then
called after her. "And don't you dare underestimate that talent again!"

Closing the door she sighed, for this was when it became

difficult, being clairvoyant. It was one thing to have told Pruden a year ago that his destiny lay with a woman with very pale blond hair; it was another to foresee cruelty, and possibly violence, for people she met only casually.

After a few minutes of thought she picked up Betsy Oliver's sketch, locked the door behind her and mounted the stairs to see her young artist landlord. "Kristan?" she called at his door.

"Open," he said, and she walked in, wincing a little at the painting mounted on his easel. His clothes, as usual, were daubed with paint, even his beard had flecks of green, but although she disliked his work—as he knew by now—he had studied in Paris as well as New York, and his work had begun to sell.

"*More* snakes," she said with a sigh, looking at the painting on his easel.

"My dear Madame Karitska," he said, "snakes and serpents have been the most hated, most worshiped of creatures on this planet. In history they've been symbols of good, evil, immortality, healing, fertility. Snakes are the *signature* of my work. And," he added with a boyish smile, "they have begun to sell, and for good prices. What can I do for you?"

"If the young woman who sketched this comes back," she said, showing him Betsy Oliver's sketch, "what can I suggest to her?"

He leaned close to look at it, not touching it with his paint-stained fingers. He said flatly, "I hate her—at *once* I hate her; she draws better than I ever could."

Madame Karitska smiled. "Yes, but if she returns, Kristan? She has no confidence, no money. . . ."

He sighed, and then with a shrug, "Then you'd better send her up to me. I have connections; I will even do my best to conceal my envy—my outrage—at such spontaneity."

Madame Karitska leaned over and placed a kiss on his cheek. "Thank you," she said, and left.

2

Pruden, reaching Number Twelve Arch Street, where the parents of the hit-and-run victim lived, found a police car already parked in front of the modest house. He was halfway up the stairs when the door opened and Sergeant O'Hare from the Fourth Precinct walked out.

"*You?*" he said in surprise.

Pruden nodded. "What's up, O'Hare?"

The Sergeant closed the door behind him and joined Pruden on the steps. "Burglary attempt here this morning." He turned and looked back at the house. "A bit hellish for them; they lost their daughter some days ago, hit-and-run accident over in the Ardsley section. That why you're here?"

"Roughly speaking, yes."

O'Hare shook his head. "Last house *I'd* choose if I were a burglar."

"You did say 'attempt'?" asked Pruden.

O'Hare nodded. "Very amateur, if you ask me. Broke in the back door by smashing the glass . . . Closet doors open, lock broken on a trunk in the hall, nothing taken. Must have heard the Cahns returning; they said they weren't gone long. Just to Mass at the church around the corner."

Frowning, Pruden said, "They insist nothing taken?"

O'Hare shrugged. "You can ask them for yourself," and with a "See ya," he returned to his squad car.

Pruden moved up the steps and rang the doorbell, and was not surprised when the man who opened the door said blankly, "*Another* policeman?"

Pruden said gently, "Not about your burglary, Mr. Cahn. I'm Detective Lieutenant Pruden. We're investigating your daughter's tragic accident and I've a few questions to add to the information we have."

The man looked beaten down, his eyes red-rimmed. He nodded and led Pruden into the living room, where his wife sat staring blankly at a television screen on which figures moved, but without sound. Pruden thought he had seen a good many living rooms such as the one the Cahns lived in: the matching sofa and two armchairs, shabby now; the rows of photographs on the mantel and on the upright piano in the corner; the oatmeal-colored wallpaper.

"He wants to ask about Darlene," he told his wife.

At once she rose, almost eagerly. "Have you found the driver yet? The man who—"

"No," he told her, "but we've found the car."

"But not the man?"

"It was a stolen car. I'm sorry, nothing more as yet."

The woman's numbness was suddenly replaced by anger. Thrusting a framed photograph at Pruden, Mrs. Cahn said, "Look at her, our only child, and now—"

It was a strong face, not a pretty one, but with fine bone structure: long dark hair, intelligent dark eyes. He felt his usual stab of pity at a young life so carelessly snuffed out.

"Such a good girl, and so talented," she told him angrily. "Sang in the church choir and sometimes played her violin with a little group here in Trafton. Chamber music." For a moment she looked bewildered. "She was so happy; she was studying at the university, giving violin lessons, and only two weeks ago became engaged to be married." She added almost proudly, "To a professor of music at the university, Professor Robert Blake. He was with her, you know, when it happened."

Pruden frowned. "Something about a dog?"

She nodded, tears in her eyes. "The professor told us she suddenly said, 'Oh Robert, that dog's hurt!' and she darted across the street and that's when . . . when . . ." She stopped to wipe her eyes. "Darlene always had such a tender heart."

"You still call him the professor," pointed out Pruden. "You didn't know him well?"

"They stopped in briefly about ten days ago," explained Mr. Cahn. "Darlene wanted us to meet him but they couldn't stay long; Darlene was playing in a concert at the university. And then of course we met again at the funeral."

"A tragedy for him, too," said Pruden. "You liked him?"

"Pleasant chap when we met him. And a musician." Mr. Cahn shrugged. "I suppose we'd hoped for some nice *young* man—he was older than we'd realized—but they certainly had music in common."

"And he was so kind at the funeral," added Mrs. Cahn.

"Told us he'd come back, bringing with him all her personal belongings."

"And he did?" inquired Pruden.

"Never had the chance," said Mrs. Cahn. "It was her roommate, Ginny Voorhees, packed everything into a trunk and shipped it to us. A little too quickly," she added bitterly. "Probably to make space for a *new* roommate." Her voice turned despairing. "If only Darlene hadn't run out into the street like that. Professor Blake said that he shouted at her to come back, but then this car shot out of nowhere—"

"I'm sorry. Very sorry," Pruden said. "But you did say that you've been sent her personal effects?"

Mr. Cahn looked anxiously at his wife and handed her a handkerchief. "Steady there, Jean," and to Pruden, "Yes, all her clothes and—"

"—and her collection," broke in Mrs. Cahn. "She loved flea markets. Her collection of china birds—miniatures, you know—and her graduation certificate and her music books, and the original piece of music she was working on—for the violin—to play at her next concert."

Pruden nodded, and with a glance at the ornate clock on the mantel said, "But I mustn't keep you any longer. We particularly wanted you to know that we've not been idle; we've found the car, and we'll certainly keep you posted on what progress we make in finding the driver."

Mr. Cahn, seeing him to the door, said sadly, "At the moment, you know, it scarcely matters who was driving that stolen car. So many crazy, wild kids—it can't bring back Darlene."

"No," admitted Pruden, "but it could keep one wild and crazy kid, as you put it, from killing someone else."

He left them to their mourning. Most of what he'd heard from the Cahns, Pruden had already known from the reports given him by the police in Trafton's suburb of Ardsley. There were no oddities except that it had not been a busy street the girl had crossed—was that what had nagged at him?—and the car had seemed to have "shot out of nowhere," as Mr. Cahn had described it, and according to two witnesses. Robert Blake's credentials were sound, except for a somewhat nomadic history: three years' study at Juilliard, two years teaching in California, three in Illinois, and three years at Ardsley University. Police were always suspicious, he reminded himself, but there seemed nothing untoward about this tragedy, except . . . He sighed, and wondered if Madame Karitska had as yet had time to examine Darlene's gold cross.

On impulse he turned down Eighth Street and stopped at the brownstone with the yellow door. She was just coming downstairs from Kristan's apartment, and was about to unlock her door when she saw Pruden.

"Oh, do come in," she told him. "I've not had time yet for your gold cross, but perhaps if you can tell me . . ." She glanced at her watch. "I've forty minutes before my next client."

"Good," he said, and once inside he proceded to tell her all the details he'd acquired: the girl's death on a quiet residential street; a description of the Cahns, and of a girl who had loved flea markets and collected china birds, who taught violin, and of the trunk with her belongings sent to them—too hastily, according to Mrs. Cahn—by her roommate; and the morning's clumsy burglary that could only add to the Cahns' misery.

Madame Karitska listened carefully and then she picked up the gold cross she'd placed on the table and held it in her hands. Seeing her close her eyes and concentrate Pruden felt awkward and embarrassed as to what he was asking of her . . . a simple hit-and-run accident, he reminded himself, and waited.

Madame Karitska was silent a long time. She said at last, opening her eyes, "I'm getting nothing about the girl Darlene. Are you quite sure this cross belonged to her?"

"Why?" asked a startled Pruden.

"I find only shadows. I wonder if she'd worn it for any length of time."

A chagrined Pruden said, "I didn't think of that. Are you getting someone else's impressions? Someone who owned it before?"

"Wait." She held up a hand. "You said she was a violinist?"

When he nodded she frowned. "Then it has to be hers, but . . . what I'm receiving—it's very strange—is simply a picture. Quite vivid." She frowned. "She must have loved it very much. A violin."

"That's not very helpful," pointed out Pruden.

"Where is it now?" she asked. "Was it sent to her parents?"

Confused, he said, "They didn't mention it, but they have a phone; I can ask. Is it important?"

"I think it important, yes."

It was fortunate that Madame Karitska could now afford a telephone. Glancing at his notes Pruden dialed the Cahns' number, and Mr. Cahn answered.

"Her violin?" he said in a puzzled voice. "No, in the trunk there was only what we told you. Why do you—"

But Pruden had already hung up. "All right, what *is* this about a violin?"

Madame Karitska said thoughtfully, "She was a violinist, but where is her violin? I feel that it is important. You say she had a roommate who packed and shipped her trunk?"

"Yes, a Ginny Voorhees, I believe."

"The violin must therefore still be at the girl's apartment. Available."

"Look," he said, "what *is* it?"

Madame Karitska was still holding the cross. "I don't know, but it is very unusual to receive only a picture, and one so vivid. The impression I'm getting now is that it matters, yes, and is of some value."

"You can't mean financially," protested Pruden. "She was at school on a scholarship, and her parents aren't rich."

"Nevertheless, the violin is important, and there is value here. You said she loved flea markets; is it possible that she found it there?"

He whistled through his teeth. "Would Darlene Cahn know a violin of value if she saw one?"

She said dryly, "If she didn't, then it is possible that someone else might. I'm sorry, but it is the only impression I receive."

Trying to absorb this Pruden said, "She could never have afforded— But she *was* a violinist. When you say 'of value' what exactly do you mean?"

She said dryly, "I can only tell you that when I lived in Antwerp I know of a Guarnerius violin, made in 1742, that was auctioned at half a million. And that was years ago."

"Half a million!" Pruden was stunned, and then, "My God, that burglary! Do you think . . . Is it possible, then, that someone was after her *violin* when they broke into the Cahns' house a few hours ago?"

She smiled. "You're the detective, not I."

"One of her students—or her roommate," mused Pruden, "Or . . ." But he felt he already knew, and at once he was at the telephone, saying, "Margolies, is Swope there? . . . Swope, pick me up at Madame Karitska's house in a plain car, and turn on the siren, we may not have much time. On the double. We're going to Ardsley."

He put down the phone, kissed Madame Karitska on the cheek and said, "I'll let you know. . . ."

The apartment was on the top floor of a shabby building that housed students, young artists and welfare people. Pruden took the stairs two at a time, with Swope stopping to catch his breath but not far behind. After he'd knocked on the door of 410 it was opened by a young girl with a mass of curly blond hair and a small round face.

"Miss Voorhees? Ginny Voorhees?"

"Yes," she said, puzzled as she looked from Pruden to Swope.

"Police," he told her, bringing out and showing her his badge.

"Police!"

"Yes, with one question to ask of you. Do you have Darlene Cahn's violin here?"

Frowning, she said, "Yes, of course. It didn't fit into the trunk. I've just been writing a note to her parents to explain, and—"

Pruden lifted her roughly out of the doorway and thrust her inside while Swope closed the door behind them. She gasped, "How dare you! You can't be the police, who are you?"

"You're sure her violin is here? It's important, and yes, we're the police and if it's not you, then we're in time; we believe someone wants that violin."

"I don't understand," she protested.

"Trust us. Where is it?"

"Over there," she told him, pointing to a shabby violin case, its exterior scuffed and worn, and added, "And it's *hers*. Darlene's dead and you have no right. I insist on verifying who you are."

"No time," Pruden said. "The Cahns had a burglary this morning and we have a strong suspicion that next their burglar will be coming here, and whoever is going to knock on your door will be after that violin."

Swope said quietly, "There's someone coming up the stairs now."

"But why? And who?"

Pruden led her away from the door to a corner of the room, where he said quietly, sternly, "This is for Darlene."

"*Darlene?*"

He nodded. "Swope and I—" He pointed to the bedroom. "Swope, carry the violin in there and hide it. That's where we'll be, too. And this is what you must do," he told her, and he spoke to her in a low voice until, hearing the knock on the door, he said, "You think you can do it?"

She said shakily, but with spirit, "I—I think so, I played Ophelia in *Hamlet* in high school. If it's for Darlene—"

"Good girl."

Leaving the bedroom door ajar Pruden and Swope waited. Ginny Voorhees, answering the knock, said with proper astonishment, "Professor Blake, it's *you?*"

An amused voice said, "When I came to pick up Darlene you always called me Robert."

Ginny gave a small laugh. "Okay—Robert. Sorry, it's been such a sad time, such a shock. I saw you at the funeral. You must miss her terribly."

"Terribly," said the man. "That's why I came, hoping she left something I can cherish as a part of her. Something to remember her by always."

Ginny Voorhees said, "I've already sent her personal belongings to her parents. She didn't have any jewelry, except of course for her engagement ring, and she was . . . well, buried wearing it, so really there's nothing."

"I meant something of hers that she valued and used every day. Her violin, perhaps."

There was silence and then Ginny Voorhees said, "But you don't play the violin, it's piano you teach."

The man's voice softened seductively. "But the violin's still here, isn't it? and I'd dearly love to have it. You know the duets we played together, what could be more personal?"

Purden hoped like hell that Ginny Voorhees wouldn't ask how he knew the violin was still here; he brought his gun out of its holster, and waited.

But Ginny Voorhees had refused that trap, and he had to admire her as she said firmly, "Yes it's here, but I really feel strongly that her parents should have it. After all, they loved her for twenty-four years, but you knew her only—"

The man's voice hardened. "Nevertheless I'd like that violin very much, Ginny."

"It's just a violin she bought at the flea market for seventy-five dollars, Robert."

"Exactly," he said. "Now go and get it. *Now.*"

"No," she told him firmly.

There was silence, and Pruden had no idea as to what was happening until Ginny Voorhees said in a steady voice, "Surely that can't be a *real* gun you just pulled out of your pocket, Robert."

"It's a real gun, and it shoots bullets," he said in a hard voice, "and I'm ready to use it. I warn you, I'll pull this trigger if you don't get her violin for me now, this minute."

"Robert, what's happened to you? You're mad, you have to be crazy."

"Crazy?" he shouted. "You think I want to go on teaching

stupid kids with no talent for the rest of my life? Damn you, it's one of Stradivari's Habeneck violins and worth a fortune, and I'll kill if I have to. Where is it?"

"I won't tell you, it's Darlene's."

"Mine now," he told her. "If you don't get it I'll find it myself."

"You'll never get away with this, Professor Blake. The police—"

"Police?" he said scornfully. "Never. You won't be alive to tell them, I'll see to that, and after all, it was just a violin bought at a flea market for seventy-five dollars. The police will never know."

It was at this moment that Pruden, who had his own flair for the dramatic, walked out of the bedroom, gun firmly in hand, to say smoothly, "But the police already know, Blake," and he had time to admire the dumbfounded look on the man's face as Swope deprived him of his pistol.

"And that," Pruden told Madame Karitska later, "is why Darlene's fiancé made no move to prevent the girl from rushing out into the street to be killed, on what pretext we'll never know. It certainly wasn't a dog . . . He knew the car was waiting up the street for that moment, and he timed it perfectly."

"And the driver of the car that hit her?"

"An ex-student of his, just out of jail and promised a very handsome sum of money to do it."

Madame Karitska, having known her share of evil, shivered.

"It still remains very strange to me, my receiving no impressions of Darlene when I held her gold cross. I can only assume that her professor had recently bought it for her and had carried it around in his pocket for several days, and it was his obsession over the violin that came through to me. An obsessed mind blocks out personality. . . . Would he have killed Ginny Voorhees, too?"

"I think he was just desperate enough to do it," said Pruden. "He never expected resistance, and he'd dreamed of what that Stradivarius would bring to him as soon as he recognized it." Pruden added wryly, "It's a pity that Ginny Voorhees teaches art or I'd have nominated her for an Academy Award for the performance she gave. Brave girl! Incidentally, the Cahns would like to meet you sometime. Naturally I told them about you."

"But I did so little," she protested.

Pruden laughed. "Then tell me how anyone else would ever have guessed that a violin was involved in her murder. If not for that, Ginny Voorhees would probably have given him what she assumed was an old flea market violin—why not? Or if it had reached the Cahns he would have made the same approach to them: something to remember her by, and then I'm sure he would have resigned from the university and moved to a distant city—California, perhaps—where he could safely sell the Stradivarius and live that life of ease he craved."

"And where is the violin now?" she asked.

"The Cahns are presenting it to the music department of the university, to be loaned out upon request. As a gift from their daughter. In her name—Darlene Cahn."

Madame Karitska nodded. "Something to remember her by."

Pruden said dryly, "Which, ironically, was just what Professor Blake wanted, too, something to remember her by which he'll have, now, for a good many years."

3

There was still no news of Georges Verlag, which troubled Madame Karitska. She had given Pruden a description of him to quietly circulate at police headquarters in case he was seen on the street, but to list him as an official missing person could only endanger him. On this morning, a mist clouding the sky after a night of rain, Pruden stopped in to tell her it would soon be time they returned the jewels, with or without Verlag. They had contacted the Manhattan police, asking them to make inquiries in the Diamond District on Forty-seventh Street between Fifth and Sixth avenues, where—among the dealers, diamond cutters, polishers, brokers, and importers—they hoped to extract information as to the European dealer for whom Georges Verlag would have been delivering his attaché case of uncut diamonds.

"I'm sorry," he told her, "sorriest for you that he's not turned up."

"I understand," she said, nodding. "It's scarcely legal for you to hold a small fortune in your safe for long."

"From New York we've learned that just such a salesman

32

was recently murdered at one of their airports, but not, fortunately, Georges Verlag. Diamonds are obviously *too* valuable and rare."

Madame Karitska said dryly, "Not so rare as people think. De Beers very cleverly holds back an enormous number of diamonds lest they flood the market and lower their price, but that's another story. . . . You look tired, you've been working too hard?"

He sank to the couch with a sigh. "Yes, damn it. What began as a case for Swope to handle has everyone in the department involved now, and yes, it adds considerably to my work. If you read the newspapers—"

She smiled faintly. "You know I don't."

He nodded. "The murder has been in the headlines for most of this week." With a glance at his watch he said, "If you still have some of your Turkish coffee handy—it's as good as a shot of brandy—maybe talking it out will stop its haunting me."

"Coffee it will be," she said, and leaving him slumped on the couch, obviously exhausted, she presently returned with carafe and a cup. "Talk," she told him, smiling, and seated herself on the couch opposite him, the low square table between them.

"Good," he said, taking a sip. "I'll make it brief; I've not much time. One of Trafton's well-known citizens—John Epworth—has been murdered under the most bizarre circumstances. Retired and wealthy, lives in a posh apartment in that high-rise on Sixty-fifth Street. Wife's name Joanna.

Since retirement Epworth had been devoting his time exclusively to charitable work at the Trafton Home for Disabled Children."

"And you say he's been *murdered?*"

He sighed. "Unfortunately and tragically, yes. The Epworths would bring one of the disabled children home to their apartment quite frequently. . . . This particular weekend it was a nine-year-old girl named Jenny. Mrs. Epworth walks into the living room on Saturday night and finds her husband lying on the floor stabbed to death with an especially lethal dagger plunged into his back—he had a collection of them mounted on his wall. Blood all over the place, the child Jenny gone, her bloody fingerprints on both dagger and doorknob. A few drops of blood in hallways. The girl had obviously fled, the bed prepared for her never slept in. Time of death, half past nine."

"A nine-year-old child!" exclaimed Madame Karitska. "Did she hate him so much? Was he unkind?"

He shook his head. "That's what's so baffling. Epworth was particularly kind to her because she resembled the daughter from his first marriage, killed with her mother in an auto accident. From all reports the child adored the Epworths, not being accustomed to such kindness, according to the people at the home. The Epworths—both of them— went out of their way to befriend Jenny . . . not the first time they'd had her for a weekend. Treats, that sort of thing."

"They've searched the building for the girl?"

He nodded. "What's difficult to understand is why nobody has seen her; she must have been splattered with blood.

There's a doorman—he could have been talking to someone, or dozing on his feet, but he insists he saw no child leaving."

"And Mrs. Epworth?"

"Distraught. Hysterical and furious. At once cut off future contributions to the Home for Disabled Children. Recklessly threatening to kill the child once found."

Madame Karitska frowned. "But how far could a physically disabled child *go*?"

"That is a problem in itself," said Pruden wearily. "She's not physically disabled, she's what I believe is called a mute. The girl can neither hear nor speak."

"Good heavens, how tragic," said Madame Karitska, startled. "Yet strong enough to kill with a dagger? What can have possessed her?"

Pruden nodded grimly. "How can one possibly guess what a child like that would feel or know if she can't talk? There's no way of knowing, not really, what hatred or resentment was seething inside of her."

"Yet she must have been likable for them to be so partial to her. How does Mrs. Epworth describe her?"

"Too grief-stricken to be coherent, but according to the people at the Home for Disabled Children, it was Mrs. Epworth who chose Jenny for the weekend. Two weekends ago it was a child in a wheelchair, this weekend Jenny. All Mrs. Epworth screams over and over is, 'To think, after all we did for her, and she *killed* him!' "

"If they were alone he wouldn't have—I hate to say this— tried to molest her?"

Pruden sighed. "Since there were no witnesses, one can't

say no to that, but there's been no history of it. Swope's interviewed every child who's spent a weekend with them; he
comes off fatherly, thoughtful, full of jokes with them;
they've taken children to the circus, movies, beach trips in
summer. . . ."

"And you can't find the child . . . but if unable to speak or
hear, surely she's learned sign language?"

Pruden sighed. "No, Epworth was arranging for just such a
teacher—the home is so *very* underfunded—but he'd not
found anyone yet." He shook his head. "And with her fingerprints everywhere—on dagger and doorknob—"

"She has to be found," Madame Karitska said. "Has to be."

He nodded. "It's been six days—no, this morning begins
seven—and if in hiding, by now she could be dead, too, if
she's had nothing to eat. We've circulated one old ID photo
the home had of her." He pulled a copy out of his pocket and
said wryly, "Just in case you see her, but it's two years old, the
photo."

It was a picture of a small, round face encircled by tight
black curls. A sweet face, thought Madame Karitska, with
huge, anxious eyes. As the eyes *would* be, she reflected, if the
child could neither hear voices, nor voice her own thoughts
and needs. "Taken two years ago," she repeated. "She must,
surely, be in that building, Pruden. It's a high-rise, you said?"

He glanced at his watch and stood up. "Fifteen floors and
basement, yes. Time for me to go, because there's another
search pending this morning, with more men, including me,
fanning out, and the chief's secured permission now from all

the absent tenants to let us search their apartments too. People on vacation or business trips. This will be the most thorough search yet."

"Then good luck and Godspeed," she told him, "and do try for a good sleep tonight or you'll wear yourself out and I shall have to worry about you. As will Jan."

Pruden grinned. "Oh, Jan already worries, but working with children at the Settlement House she especially worries about a child in hiding, cold and hungry, whatever she may have done."

Madame Karitska glanced again at the circular he'd left on the table. "Please—let me know if you find her, will you?"

"I promise," he said, and with a last sip of coffee and a vague salute he opened the door and was gone.

It was late evening when the phone rang, and Madame Karitska knew at once that it would be Pruden. She said, "You've found Jenny?"

He said grimly, "In the basement of the building, living on garbage and sleeping in an empty garbage container, her dress stained with dried blood. I told you she was mute?"

"Yes," said Madame Karitska.

He added angrily, "And now we find we had no idea what being mute *really* meant. Swope asks questions; she can't hear them. More questions, she can't answer them. Somehow I thought she would be able to read lips, manage *something*, shake her head yes or no, but impossible when she can't *hear*."

"What about Mrs. Epworth? There must have been some way she and her husband communicated with her."

She could hear his sigh over the phone. "Under her doctor's care, heavily sedated—tranquilizers and sleeping pills . . . we have to wait. In the meantime we've got this terrified child and—"

"Still terrified?" asked Madame Karitska.

"As well as dehydrated and undernourished. She's with a children's agency for the night, but how we're ever going to learn what possessed her to turn violent and kill I don't know. Mrs. Epworth might have a clue but we can't see her yet, doctor's orders."

"Pruden," said Madame Karitska thoughtfully.

"Yes?"

She was silent and then, "I *might* be able to help. If, for instance, there is the bloodstained dress available."

"Help," he repeated, and then, "My God, yes, do you think, really think, a *dress*?"

"There could—*might*—still be a way," she told him.

He whistled through his teeth. "I should have thought of that. Whether the chief would allow . . . the dress is under lock and key, but if he'd allow . . . you might have to come to headquarters?"

"I'd be glad to," she told him.

"Great. I'll see what I can arrange, and get back to you in the morning. But I thought you'd sleep better, knowing she's been found."

"Indeed I shall," she said. "Until tomorrow, then."

The next day, at fifteen minutes before one o'clock, Swope called for her in a police car and drove her across town to headquarters.

"The chief's in a foul mood," he warned her. "Of course he knows about you now, but he doesn't *want* to know about you. Too embarrassing."

"Quite understandable," said Madame Karitska.

Headquarters was a monolithic brick building in the center of town, next to City Hall, and they discreetly entered from the rear parking lot. Swope led her down a maze of halls to an elevator, passing numerous offices, and at last to the chief. He, too, seemed rather monolithic to Madame Karitska: a large man, ruddy-faced, who had risen to his position through the ranks.

Pruden was already there, and drew up a chair for her facing the chief, while he and Swope took nearby chairs and sat down, waiting.

The child's dress lay on the desk between her and the chief. "All right," he growled, "how's this done? She talks to herself, this mute child?"

Being only too accustomed to skepticism, and to antagonism, Madame Karitska explained, "I can only pick up what she was *feeling*. Since she has her sight she would have seen words, but never knowing what they mean. Yet she's worn this smock for six days and nights, and it's possible it may tell me something. Reactions. Anger. But not in words, although it's possible she's created some sort of primitive vocabulary of her own."

He shrugged. "Sorry. I know what you all did when Pruden's fiancée was taken hostage." He sighed. "Go ahead," and to the stenographer, "Take this down, will you?" He handed Madame Karitska the unadorned smock that was brown with dried blood. "See what you can do."

"Thank you."

Pruden gave her an understanding smile, and she sat back and fingered the dress lightly, then placed it across her cupped hands and closed her eyes. In a distant room a telephone rang, followed by silence.

Pruden was surprised to see tears in Madame Karitska's eyes. She said in a shaken voice, "Dear God, this poor child."

Impatiently the chief said, "Scarcely a poor child when she kills her benefactor."

Madame Karitska held up her hand to silence him. "Please, I'm getting some very strong impressions. . . . she sits comfortably next to a 'he-person,' she calls him, a flood of happiness, feeling his warmth. I have the impression they look at pictures in a book. . . . I feel—*she* feels his kindness."

She stopped, frowning. "Then someone enters the room, scarcely noticed—"

Madame Karitska shuddered and Pruden looked at her inquiringly.

"A she-person to her," she said. "This she-person has entered the room and the child looks up. The she-person stands behind the seated man and is holding 'one of the sharp things from the wall—' "

"The daggers," broke in Pruden. "Epworth had a collection of daggers on the wall."

"—and she pushes it into the he-person's back."

"Impossible," protested the chief. "Impossible."

Madame Karitska paid him no attention. "The man falls forward, facedown on the floor—is this true? Did he? The child—Jenny—throws herself across his bleeding back, making guttural moaning sounds, pulling and tugging at him to bring him back to the couch, not understanding. I feel her shock and grief. This she-person—this woman—pulls her to her feet, places the knife in the child's now-bloody hand, then drops it on the floor and pulls her to the door, where she is forced to turn the knob with her bloody hand. The she-person mouths a word the child can't hear but knows she's being shoved out, the door closes behind her and, bewildered and frightened the girl runs down the stairs—many, many stairs—into darkness. Is it the basement? She hides there, in the darkness."

There was a long and incredulous silence following this until the chief said, "What woman? There was no woman except—"

"Except Mrs. Epworth," Swope said in a stunned voice. "You're implying that Mrs. Epworth killed her husband and deliberately used a helpless child to conceal it?"

"Could this possibly be true?" demanded the chief. "You've met her, what's she like?"

Swope nodded. "I've met her—under the worst of circumstances, of course—when completely hysterical. Attractive, younger than I expected—mid-forties, I'd guess. Mrs. Hobson at the Home for Disabled Children said she was very charming, devoted to her husband and enthusiastic about his charity work."

Pruden said, "If it *should* be true you've got to admit it would be a damn clever murder, using a witness like Jenny who can't tell anyone what she saw, or protect herself if accused." He frowned. "Swope, look at your notes again; didn't you say that Mrs. Hobson, the director at the Home for Disabled Children, told you that Mrs. Epworth specifically asked for Jenny to stay that weekend? She *insisted* on Jenny, didn't she?"

Swope nodded. "That's true. My God, if that's why— But how fiendish if . . . if—"

Madame Karitska said, "Fiendish, yes."

Frowning, the chief said, "If we believe this, surely there had to be another woman there, a maid, a cook? I can't believe—"

Swope interrupted him to say, "We checked all that, sir. Maid left at five, the cook at six. Mrs. Epworth . . ." He took out his notebook again. "She was in the kitchen—she said—at the counter, making out recipes to give the cook for a party later in the week. A party planned," he added dryly, "to elicit more contributions for the Home for Disabled Children."

"But this is unbelievable," said the chief. "Why would Mrs. Epworth—what possible motive could she have?"

Swope shook his head. "We never looked into that, sir, never dreamed—it was taken for granted, assumed—I mean, there was all that blood and Mrs. Epworth distraught, hysterical, the blood on the doorknob, the child gone and leaving a trail of blood in the hall."

"If this is true," said the chief, looking dazed, "if this *should* be true, deliberately using a disabled child to cover her

crime, she would deserve to be hanged." Startled, he added,
"Sorry, damn it; forget I said that."

"Forgiven," said Madame Karitska with a smile.

Pruden said slowly, "But if true—how clever, how shrewd.
It would be the perfect crime, wouldn't it? Absolutely the
perfect crime."

"Swope," said the chief in a hard voice, "drop everything
you're working on, and start checking out Mrs. Epworth's
past; check Epworth's will, see if Mrs. Karitska—sorry, *Madame* Karitska's right, impossible as it seems, damn it. Start
from the beginning, a fresh inquiry." To Madame Karitska he
said angrily, "If you're wrong—"

"That," said Pruden, "is for us to find out, isn't it?"

Madame Karitska rose from her chair to say quietly, "I'll go
now, but I do hope, in the meantime, the child Jenny can be
given happier surroundings while you investigate." Picking
up her purse she nodded to Pruden and Swope and left the
chief to cope with his confusion and his shock. But he was a
good man, Pruden had always said so, and she could be certain that he would be thorough.

4

Pruden, joining Swope the next morning for their new assignment, said, "The hell of it is, if Madame Karitska should be right about Mrs. Epworth, how can there be any possibility of proving her guilty and the child innocent, with Jenny's bloody fingerprints all over the dagger and door?"

Swope nodded. "I've had time to realize that, too. A lot of footwork ahead, and dare I add that it comes down to a test of Madame Karitska's clairvoyance? She's been right about a helluva lot of things but can anyone be a hundred percent right all the time? I can't, just can't believe—"

"Let's just get started," Pruden said grimly. "It's not going to be easy."

They decided it was best not to approach Epworth's lawyer about the will yet, there being no rational explanation to give him for any inquiry. Not yet, at least, with Mrs. Epworth still under a doctor's care. City Hall first, maiden name at marriage, hopefully an old address or two . . . "Married how long?" asked Pruden.

"Eight years."

By noon they'd learned that Mrs. Epworth's maiden name was Joanna Warren, and at the time of her marriage she'd lived at 29 Cozzen Street in Trafton. In the basement of the *Trafton Times* they pored over accounts of the wedding; the bride was a native of New York City, and private secretary to Mr. Epworth's partner at the Epworth-Bartlett Company. With birth date and birthplace established they repaired to computers at headquarters but learned very little, except for the fact that she'd been ticketed twice for speeding, and was born in Brooklyn.

About Joanna Warren Epworth as a living, breathing person they learned nothing. Apparently once she married a well-known and successful financier the personality became obscured, decided Pruden, and what they needed was to learn who she had once been, and hope to meet the present Joanna in a day or two.

This left 29 Cozzen Street, where someone might possibly remember her, even after so many years. "Highly doubtful," Swope agreed.

Twenty-nine Cozzen Street was a modest apartment house on a tree-lined street at the edge of town, and here they met with a modicum of luck. The superintendent had been there for years, and he did remember her.

"Stunning blonde," he said. "Attracted men like flies. But nice."

"And would there be anyone in the building now who knew her when she lived here?"

He thought a moment, frowning. "It being rent-controlled,

most tenants have been here a long time. Miss Jacoby would be the one to see . . . Miss Abby Jacoby. Lived next to her, and close friends, if I remember rightly."

"Would she be here now? What apartment number?"

"Thirty-two," he said. "She comes and goes, what you call a buyer. New York. The department stores, you know? Think she came back last night."

"Thanks," said Pruden, and they headed for apartment 32 and rang the buzzer.

Abby Jacoby opened the door to them in pajamas and a robe, a vivacious-looking fortyish woman, slim as a reed, her shingled hair an attractive and unembarrassed silvery gray. "Oh, limey," she said with a grin, "the police, and me in pajamas in daylight!"

It was impossible not to smile back at her.

"Come in, come in," she said. "I always take a day off after a week in New York . . . nobody in the fashion business seems to go to bed until the sun comes up."

Without the slightest self-consciousness she sat herself on the arm of a chair and said, "Okay, what have I done?"

Swope grinned. "Strictly a routine inquiry, Miss Jacoby. Have you happened to see the Trafton newspapers since you returned?"

"Just call me Abby," she told them, and then, "Oh my gosh, Joanna's husband! I came in last night and turned on the news . . . only the tail end of it. Eulogies, and all that about him, I suppose that means he's dead?" Swope nodded. "Poor Joanna."

"Have you remained friends?" asked Pruden.

"Are you kidding? No, we were good friends when she lived here, but she went her merry way. I have to admit I was startled when I read of her marrying Mr. Epworth."

"Why?" asked Swope.

She looked from one to the other and said, "Look, what's this all about?"

Pruden weighed his words carefully. He could think of several subterfuges but decided that none of them would fool this woman. "Mrs. Epworth is under sedation and can't be interviewed yet. In the meantime we're making inquiries into everyone who knew the couple. Mr. Epworth, you see, was murdered."

"Good heavens," she said, shocked, and then, "I can tell you right now if Joanna's a suspect you'd be barking up the wrong tree. Marriage to Mr. Epworth would have been just what she wanted—I don't mean that in any nasty way—but it made absolute sense for her."

"Can you explain that?" asked Swope.

Abby Jacoby shrugged. "You'd have to know her, of course. She was quite fun, and we double-dated a lot. . . . Enviably beautiful, of course." She sighed. "And I admit she knew how to use it. She'd been a model but she wanted something more *useful*. She was tremendously efficient and wasn't *using* herself, she said, which is why she moved uptown. And then there was Rick, of course," she added, frowning.

"Rick?"

She nodded. "Rick O'Hara." She sighed. "I *know* she cared about him, and he adored her and wanted to marry her. What a handsome couple they were, but you know how opposites attract? She was all ambition and he was . . . well, easygoing. An accountant, dreaming of a ranch out west." She smiled, remembering. "She couldn't persuade him to become a CPA— certified public accountant—or *anything* to get ahead. He just laughed. I think marrying him scared her."

"Scared her?"

She nodded. "She said, growing up poor, it scared her. She always seemed to have this picture in her mind of how it had been growing up, her mother scrubbing floors for a living, pinching pennies. When I think about it, I wasn't *that* surprised when I read about her marriage to Mr. Epworth. She did everything so well, she would have been great, cutting ribbons and heading committees. I think that's why she broke it off with Rick. I *know* she cared about him, but—I know it wasn't easy for her, but Rick wasn't . . . well, ambitious at all. Just easygoing, charming, and happy as he was."

"You've not seen her since she left?"

She shook her head. "I could understand her cutting me off; I would have reminded her of Rick. I don't know whether she ever got over it, but . . ." She smiled wryly. "At least she didn't have to pinch pennies. And she would have been a very efficient and faithful wife, I'm sure."

"And what happened to Rick?" asked Swope curiously.

"I think it broke his heart when they split. I heard he did a lot of drinking and then he pulled his life together, married, and moved out west somewhere."

Swope snapped his notebook closed. "You've been very frank and open with us, Miss Jacoby, and we appreciate it." With a glance at Pruden, "Time we go now, isn't it?"

Pruden nodded. "Thank you very much, Miss Jacoby. Or Abby," he added.

She rose from her seat and said, "Look, when Joanna's over the shock, tell her Abby says hello and sends her sympathies, will you?"

Very gravely Pruden assured her that yes, they would deliver her message, and they left, but still with no idea or clue as to who or what Mrs. Epworth had become eight years later.

Pruden didn't usually talk about his work with Jan, but that afternoon he visited her at the Settlement House where she worked, and he confided to her their dilemma.

His very dear fiancée was always perceptive. "What you *really* need," she told him, after hearing his story, "is reassurance that Marina Karitska's bizarre description of what happened is true."

He admitted to this. "But we're up against a child who can't defend herself, or explain anything that happened, or what she heard."

"It's not hopeless," said Jan firmly. "We've a child psychologist on call at the Settlement House, Lou Devoe, who does things with pictures and dolls. She's very good; I'll phone her. Her office is downtown; there's even a window through which you can watch what she does if the child, Jenny—you said her name is Jenny?—could be taken there."

"Jan," he said, his spirits lifting, "you continue to be a miracle in my life."

She said with a smile, "Doubt Marina Karitska if you must, but try to keep in mind just who it was who predicted that we'd meet—and long before we did."

"Touché," he said with a grin. "I'll take this up with the chief at once. Give me this psychiatrist's address and phone number, and could you call and tell her we just may get clearance for this?"

For her trip to the psychiatrist someone had given Jenny a shabby dress that hung on her unbecomingly. She was escorted to the office by a policewoman who had mercifully forsworn her uniform lest it frighten the child. Dr. Louise Devoe was all warmth, greeting Jenny, and the matron was banished behind the one-way glass window with Pruden and Swope. From here they could observe what looked more like a playroom than an office, and for Jenny there were dolls of all shapes and sizes, and several stuffed animals to hold.

It was tiresome, watching, but it rested Pruden to see the tense and frightened child slowly relax and embrace dolls while Dr. Devoe smiled, nodded, and gave her an occasional affectionate hug. After a while the matron left, asking them to call when the appointment was over.

They had been at the window for over an hour before Dr. Devoe brought out two small doll-like figures—a man and a child—and then a miniature couch. She set the father figure on the couch, the child next to him, and for the first time Jenny smiled. Jenny patted the man, and moved the child-doll a little closer to him, pleased. Dr. Devoe nodded encouragingly—she seemed capable of relating to Jenny on some subconscious level—and waited before she introduced the figure of the doll in a dress. Seeing the woman-doll Jenny stopped smiling. Dr. Devoe handed it to her with an understanding nod, as if to ask where to place the woman in this family scene. Jenny hesitated and then stood the woman behind the tiny couch. After a moment, with an angry guttural sound, she grasped the doll-woman and with it struck the man, and sending him to the floor she burst into tears. Her sobs racked her; she picked up the fallen man-doll and hugged it closely as Dr. Devoe put her arms around her to comfort her.

"It wouldn't stand up in court," Dr. Devoe told Pruden and Swope later, "but I'd say that she definitely re-created the scene you'd come to expect—or to investigate as possibility."

Madame Karitska, then, could be believed, thought Pruden, and this very much relieved and satisfied him. It was time to learn who represented the Epworths legally, he decided, and change the direction of their inquiries.

The Epworths' lawyer, they discovered, was Everett Harbinger of Benson and Harbinger on State Street, and the next morning, with their appointment made, they waited in two chairs, a table of magazines between them, before they were ushered into Mr. Harbinger's office. He proved to be a tall thin man with a tired face but penetrating eyes as he looked them over.

"So," he said, glancing at the two cards they had sent in to him. "Detective Lieutenant Pruden, and Detective Swope. How can I help you?"

"We're investigating the death of John Epworth," Pruden told him.

"Investigating? *Still?*" he said dryly. "You surprise me."

Very politely Pruden said, "Detectives, like lawyers, want to be thorough. To poke and pry, so to speak, into the 'why' of this tragedy. You knew John Epworth well?"

"*Very* well. We've been good friends for a long time," he said. "Especially when Jean was alive. His first wife," he explained. "Lovely woman. Her death was a great shock to him—to us all—and of course the child was in the car, too."

Pruden nodded. "Like many people in Trafton I admired him but we know so little of the situation, Mrs. Epworth being under a doctor's care and unapproachable. You've met his second wife, of course."

He shrugged. "Only at social affairs. She shone at those."

Pruden, with what he hoped sounded like normal curiosity, said, "I take it that she is not very much like Mr. Epworth's first wife?"

"Good God, no," said Harbinger.

Pruden smiled. "I take it you don't appreciate her."

"I thought her much too interested in John's money. And in spending it," he added. "When we golfed together John would joke about it but he didn't seem to mind; he was always generous. No, I thought that marriage a big mistake. No warmth in her."

"Of course," pointed out Pruden carefully, "she will have full control of his money now that he's dead?"

Harbinger gave him a long and thoughtful glance. "Just why are you here?" he asked. "And investigating? You're surely not implying . . . not suggesting . . . That is, according to the newspapers, John's murder has already been solved, publicized, and is virtually ready for trial."

"Not to us," Pruden said calmly, and took an enormous chance by saying quietly, "You could be of tremendous help to us if we could learn about Mr. Epworth's will that you drew up for him."

Harbinger looked amused. "You know I can't allow that, it would be highly unethical."

"Yes," agreed Pruden, "but wouldn't it also be unethical to see an innocent child condemned?"

This startled him. "You can't be serious," he insisted. "I began my career as a defense attorney and I certainly don't envy the lawyer appointed to defend that unfortunate possessed child. It's a watertight case."

"We don't believe that," Pruden told him.

Harbinger frowned. "I can't think of anything more unethical than to share information that's highly confidential."

Pruden nodded. "That's understood. Couldn't we call it simply an exchange of important information, information that I sincerely believe John Epworth would approve, considering what's at stake?"

Harbinger sighed. "If you really think . . . All right, I'll tell you this much: John was about to make a few changes in his will. Two weeks ago an appointment was made for . . ." He glanced at his calendar. "For later this week. This Friday, when he and his wife were to meet me here to—as he put it— update his will. Minor changes, he said."

"May we ask what changes he wanted made?" inquired Swope.

"He didn't say. He was always a very generous man, and of course very wealthy, so I assumed that he wanted to include a few charities in a new will. I think what you want to know is whether the will, made out at the time of his second marriage, left his entire fortune to his wife. It did, yes."

"I see," murmured Pruden.

"However," continued Harbinger, "shortly after making that Friday appointment he asked to see me privately to discuss the changes he'd considered. He came alone, explaining that he preferred to come alone because after much thought he'd reached the decision that he wanted very *major* changes made, wanted his money divided in half. Half to his wife, and half to the Trafton Home for Disabled Children. Does this surprise you?"

Pruden didn't answer that but said, "Just how would that change in his will break down, moneywise?"

"Fifteen million to his wife, fifteen million to the home, which had become much more than a hobby for him. He seemed truly committed to helping them. Gave me the impression that he felt it was very creative and meaningful for him; the home was sadly underfunded and its buildings rundown. He spoke of the need for more hearing aids, a teacher to teach sign language, he wanted to see the playground expanded, more wheelchairs added, and he wanted the money placed in a fund to be drawn on year by year."

"And did his wife agree to this?" asked Pruden. "He'd talked about it with her?"

Harbinger's eyes narrowed. "I had the impression that he'd tried to talk about it with her, but she was—or so I gathered—quite upset about it, and this troubled him. I think it troubled him very much. She knew, of course, of the appointment he'd made for them both this Friday and she had assumed the changes to be minor; she'd had no idea that he'd suddenly decided on such a drastic change." He paused, and then, "This interests you?"

"Very much," said Pruden. "You know it does. But he never changed the will, then; he deferred to his wife's anger?"

"Which is why you're here, of course," said Harbinger. "But if it's a matter of justice . . . Actually when he came to see me that day, without his wife, he changed his will, and that will is now in my safe-deposit box. He also wanted to keep tomorrow's appointment on my calendar, from which I deduced that he'd not told his wife what he'd done, but preferred to tell her of the change—to avoid a scene, perhaps—when they arrived here on Friday. He said it meant a great deal to him to use the money he'd made as he chose, and for something *useful*."

"He didn't like scenes," murmured Swope.

"No man does."

"And now he's dead," said Pruden. "Did you entertain no . . . shall we say, no *suspicions*?"

"Under different circumstances, yes," said Harbinger. "One would have to admit that his death arrived at a most convenient time for Joanna, but there was so much evidence, and every indication . . . that angry child leaving her fingerprints all over the apartment and fleeing, and surely you have no evidence otherwise?" He frowned. "I've been frank with you, at the risk of my integrity; now it's time you level with me. *Have* you evidence to suggest otherwise?"

"Yes and no," Pruden told him with a frown. "That is to say, any evidence we have would never stand up in court."

Harbinger's eyes probed them both. "Provocative but in-conclusive. Do you mind telling me what *you* think might have happened?"

Pruden exchanged doubtful glances with Swope, but Harbinger, without waiting for a reply, turned to his intercom. "Miss Dotson," he said, "no calls for the next forty minutes, if you please. I am in conference."

The next morning Pruden and Swope were told that Mrs. Epworth could at last be interviewed. For days their approach had met with rebuffs from her doctor, but now, although she was grief-stricken, the doctor said she was no longer under sedation and could describe for them the harrowing events of the week before, and answer any ques-tions they had about the child Jenny. She was, however, very fragile still.

Pruden said smoothly, "Of course. So far we have only the police report given on the night of the murder. If she could fill in some details we'd appreciate it. What hour would be convenient?"

It was agreed that at two o'clock that afternoon they could meet with her at her apartment, and Pruden at once put in a call to Everett Harbinger at Benson and Harbinger, and alerted Swope, who would meet him there. Pruden preferred to walk, and on his way to Sixty-ninth Street he found him-self increasingly curious about this Joanna Warren Epworth. In his early days on the force, when on patrol duty and as-signed to crowd control, he'd frequently seen John Epworth, and he'd liked the look of him. He'd been told that since the accident that claimed the life of his wife and child years ago, he'd given himself entirely to business and civic matters, but, as Pruden saw it, a man like that might keep hoping to find a woman to match the wife he'd lost so tragically. As the years passed and he realized the impossibleness of this, and feeling his mortality, he could easily be drawn to someone twenty years younger who flattered him, made him feel younger, and revived the nurturing qualities that he'd buried. He wondered if this second Mrs. Epworth would be what he called the second-marriage sort: flawlessly attractive—his wealth would assure that—and the type who would, as Abby Jacobs had suggested, look good at board meetings, and efficiently build a social life for him. Now Pruden would finally meet her, this woman who might just have efficiently arranged what she would believe the perfect crime.

Swope was silent when they met; he didn't like this any more than Pruden. They rang the bell, and a maid in uniform escorted them into a living room full of antiques. They gingerly chose two elegant chairs and sat, waiting.

Mrs. Epworth entered the room wearing black silk slacks and a black silk shirt, her face very pale, and Pruden noted with professional interest that she wore no makeup, and wondered if she'd sacrificed vanity to emphasize her mourning. She chose a very straight chair and smiled wanly. "I believe you want more . . . details?"

Pruden said, "We've taken the liberty of asking your lawyer to join us. He should be here at any moment."

He had startled her. "Whatever for?" she said lightly. "Surely not some Victorian idea that I'd need *protection*."

Lying through his teeth, Pruden said, "It's regulations, our policy at headquarters, Mrs. Epworth, that in every criminal case a lawyer must be present to protect the interest of anyone interviewed."

But the maid was already ushering in Mr. Harbinger, and rising to greet him she lifted both arms in a dramatic and helpless gesture. "What a waste of your time, Everett," she told him. "They think I need protection."

Harbinger smiled. "Ah, but this also gives me the opportunity to later go over John's will with you before it's filed with probate."

She brightened. "Oh, how very efficient of you. Do sit down, all of you," and to Harbinger, "You have the will with you?"

Harbinger smiled charmingly. "Yes, indeed, making you a very wealthy woman . . ." Which, thought Pruden, was true enough, finding fifteen million a very nice fortune. Fumbling with his attaché case Harbinger said with sympathy, "And what are your plans now?"

Both were ignoring Pruden and Swope. Speaking directly to Harbinger she said with passion, "Oh, to get *away*." They'd not noticed the handkerchief crumpled in one hand; she lifted it now to dab at each eye. "I can't tell you how terrible it's been, Everett. I'm worn out; I need a rest badly."

He nodded understandingly. "A spa, perhaps?" he suggested, still groping in his attaché case.

She shook her head. "The south of France might be restful—perhaps I'll buy a villa there. I could afford that. My nerves . . . I've been under sedation for days, you know, and the doctor urges a complete change of scene, it's been such a terrible shock." Again she dabbed at her eyes. "It's been heartrending."

Harbinger nodded sympathetically. "You'll sell this apartment?"

She nodded, and touched her eyes again, very delicately, with the handkerchief. "It would be unbearable now."

"Trafton will miss you," he said politely.

"I'd keep the condominium in Manhattan, of course." She was thoughtful a moment, and then, "How much estate tax will there be on thirty million, Everett?"

Harbinger said smoothly, "You will have to consult your accountant about that, but you mistake the amount that you'll inherit; it will be fifteen million, not thirty million."

"Fifteen!" she said sharply, too sharply, and covered this with a quick smile. "You have to be mistaken, the will that we made eight years ago left me thirty million."

"The will of eight years ago, yes," said Harbinger, "but that has been changed, you see."

"Changed! Changed?" She stared at him incredulously. "I don't believe it; how can you say that? John couldn't— There were to be some adjustments made, yes, and we were to see you—tomorrow, wouldn't it be?"

"True." Harbinger nodded. "But ten days ago your husband came alone to my office to make those so-called adjustments, to make them himself. A matter of conscience, no doubt. I believe he'd already discussed it with you, dividing his estate."

"What?" She gasped. "But I told him no—absolutely not,

that it wouldn't be fair. You're saying that he did that in spite of— No, John would never do that to me, it's impossible."

"I'm sure you recall what he discussed with you," Harbinger pointed out. "He leaves fifteen million to you, fifteen to the Trafton Home for Disabled Children."

"But that's *cruel!*" she cried. "It's not fair. That awful place with those depressing cripples?" Too angry to notice their shocked faces she said, "It's Jenny—retarded, surely—who murdered him. It's insane, she killed him, she drove that terrible dagger into him with such *force*, and to leave his money—"

Pruden interrupted to say politely, "I believe you told the police that night that you were in the kitchen; you couldn't possibly have learned with what force—"

"I mean I *heard* it," she said, momentarily confused but defiant. "I *heard* it," and turning to Harbinger, "How could you let my husband do this to me, change the will like that, without me there. How *could* you! I'm his *wife*."

"As I said before, a matter of conscience?" suggested Harbinger.

"I'll sue," she flung at him angrily, eyes glittering, no longer a bereaved widow now.

Harbinger said dryly, "I really doubt that any judge or jury would find you deprived when he'd left you fifteen million."

She stared at him in shock, and then at Pruden and Swope. If she had expected sympathy she found none, and there was the faintest hint of her beginning to unravel. "But you can't do this," she protested, and there were tears in her eyes.

The shock of her husband's betrayal was obviously a blow but Pruden wondered what dreams and plans for that thirty million had driven her; whatever it was, it was shattering that masklike poise and confidence. Fifteen million wasn't enough; she'd unwittingly made it obvious that she'd never shared her husband's interest in his charities, and possibly not even in her husband, John Epworth. *She's a hard woman under that facade,* he realized, *but not hard enough,* and he shrank at what lay ahead.

"You can't do this," she repeated, tears staining her cheeks. "John would never have done such a thing. If he was alive—"

"But he isn't alive," said Pruden, "and Jenny didn't kill him."

"Are you mad?" she said wonderingly. "Of course she did, she was there, I told you so. Who else could have killed him?"

"You," said Pruden.

"*What?*" she gasped. "How dare you! Everett, are you going to allow him to say such a thing to me? There *can't* be any such evidence."

"Why not?" asked Harbinger pleasantly.

"Why not?" she echoed. "Because Jenny's a mute, she can't talk, she can't hear, I made sure of—" She stopped, appalled, and pressed a fist to her mouth. "You weren't there; how could you think—"

"You removed the dagger from your husband's body," said Pruden steadily, "and you made sure that Jenny's bloodied fingerprints were placed on it. A helpless child who could never deny your accusation."

"*No!*" she shouted, "how can you *know* that? You can't say such a thing, I won't let you, I won't listen, I have plans and you've no right—"

"Enough evidence," continued Pruden, hating himself for this, "to convict you of very cleverly using Jenny to conceal that it was you who killed your husband."

"I'm not listening," she told him furiously. "What evidence could you possibly have? I won't listen."

"Enough evidence," lied Pruden.

"No," she cried. "Impossible! Jenny can't talk; Jenny's a mute. Everett—" She turned to him, but seeing his impassive face she burst into tears. "I can't bear this; it wasn't supposed to be like this. Everett, it *has* to be Jenny, don't you see?" she pleaded. "Tell them it's Jenny; tell them I have *plans.*"

"What plans?" Harbinger asked gently.

"I wanted . . . I wanted—" She stopped, confused and dazed, her lips trembling. "I had *plans,*" she repeated, and Harbinger, a look of pity on his face, went to the telephone and put in a call to her doctor.

"And that's how it ended," Pruden told Madame Karitska that night. "Not a pretty story."

"Where is she now?"

He sighed. "In a psychiatric hospital. She insists that she's Joanna Warren and never knew a John Epworth; she seems to have completely blotted out the last eight years. Strange, isn't it?"

Madame Karitska shook her head. "Not so strange," she said. "From what her friend Abby told you she was very likable in those days, ambitious but likable. I would guess that she can't face what she's become and what she did."

He nodded. "She must have felt like Cinderella when John Epworth proposed marriage to her." He stopped and then added sadly, "My guess is that she learned money was no substitute for love, and with no grounds for divorce she began dreaming of being a rich young widow in the south of France, and finding love at last with a husband her own age." He shrugged. "But we'll never know."

He suddenly smiled. "Ironically, there's one happy note to add to this story of vanity and greed. . . . John Epworth had at last found a teacher of sign language shortly before his death. She arrived at the home yesterday, and it's hoped that in a few weeks, a month at most, Jenny will have learned enough to verify our evidence.

"That evidence," he added dryly, "that we only hoped we had, but could never have proved in court."

5

The next morning Madame Karitska saw three clients in succession and then, with Georges Verlag still on her mind, she made a brief phone call to a man by the name of Amos Herzog.

"My dear Countess," he said, "come at once. I have just completed writing my chapter on Earnestine Boulanger, who poisoned three husbands, and she has proved the most boring woman I've spent a week with. It would be a pleasure to see you, but *not*," he added dryly, "with that policeman friend of yours. I remain, still, allergic to the police."

She laughed. "No, I'm still saving you for a surprise. This concerns diamonds, and I'll be there in fifteen minutes."

Leaving a sign on her door, BACK AT 2 PM, she walked to the subway and was soon strolling down Cavendish Square with its stately homes and gardens. Number 46, however, housed elegant apartments where Amos occupied the first floor. It amused her very much that decades ago Amos Herzog had been the country's most outrageously successful jewel thief, moving in the best of circles—as he still did—and had been famous for never carrying a gun during his robberies. Very

64

sensibly he had retired after two stints in jail, and for years had been writing a series of books on—of all things—famous crimes in history. If there were some who wondered how his modest book sales supported a luxurious apartment on Cavendish Square, if they perhaps wondered if he had stashed away many of his ill-gotten gains in Switzerland, he was so charming, and so often of help to the FBI—he had even taught a class for them on picking locks—that no one cared enough to explore the source of his income . . . so long as he remained retired.

That he had actually been a client of hers a few months after she'd hung out her sign still amused her. Not many Mercedeses were to be seen on Eighth Street, and his astonishment when she'd opened her door had been palpable. "Good God," he'd said.

Out of desperation, irritation, and condescension he'd either heard of her or seen her sign, and apparently had decided that she was his last but no doubt vain hope. He had lost or mislaid a coin in his apartment.

"Not a valuable one," he'd explained. "Worth no more than two hundred dollars, but it's been my lucky charm. I count on it, depend on it, and I can't tell you how unlucky I've been since it disappeared."

"Stolen?" she'd suggested. "Surely stolen?"

He had vigorously shaken his head. "Impossible. It has to be in my apartment, which I've ransacked, trying to find it. Too stupid of me—and certainly not a police matter. I simply wondered—"

"Tell me about it," she'd said. "Or better still, draw me a sketch of it."

He'd drawn a picture of it for her: a *real*, one of the coins commonly known as "pieces of eight," salvaged by divers from pirate ships. "Of value only to me, *always* I carried it on my person. Jacket or trouser pockets."

She nodded. "Then may I first hold something of yours, worn on your person for a number of years?"

He had never heard of psychometry, and with a laugh he'd handed her his gold signet ring.

She held it for quite a while, increasingly amused. "You have a strong sense of mischief," she told him. "And have at one time been famous—or perhaps infamous?"

"All this you pick up from a mere ring?"

"Emanations," she'd explained. "Thoughts. Moods, feelings. So much is invisible. . . . We all possess a magnetic field, a current that runs through us and that can be detected . . . when you leave that chair, for instance, yours will remain behind you for some moments." She added politely, "I have the impression that you've spent some time in . . . jail, dare I say?"

"You unman me," he'd said. "Yes, there was a time when I divested a number of wealthy matrons of their jewelry. Without violence, I can assure you."

"Ah—a jewel thief!"

"A *distinguished* jewel thief," he emphasized.

"About your missing good-luck charm . . ." She picked up his sketch to concentrate on it. "How many rooms in your house?"

"Apartment. Five."

In her mind, concentrating on the coin's picture, she went through each room. "A closet," she said at last.

"Impossible," he told her. "Sorry, I've searched every closet. Thoroughly. Every drawer, every chair, bed, and couch."

Paying no attention to this she added, "I gain an impression of fur."

"Fur!"

"Yes, have you a fur coat or rug, perhaps? No," she amended, "something *much* smaller."

"Small? And fur?" With a frown he said, "That's strange; I've a pair of very old fur bedroom slippers."

She nodded. "Good. I believe you will find the coin in one of those fur slippers, although one must wonder how it got there."

Startled, he said, "I nearly threw them away, but . . . yes, I did wear them one very cold evening a month ago. You really think . . . ?"

She laughed. "Then how fortunate you did *not* throw them away."

Surprised and curious about her, she had brewed coffee and they had settled down to a long and interesting talk about his career and hers, and by the time he left they had established an easy and amusing relationship. Not having a telephone as yet he had sent her by mail the next day a note to say the coin had been found precisely where she'd said he would find it, and he had enclosed a check, begging her to use the money to install a telephone because writing notes bored him, and he would like to talk to her occasionally.

She had not ordered a phone; she had paid her rent with his check.

Now he opened the door for her at once, still handsome and distinguished in his seventies; he had cultivated a white goatee to match his white hair, and there was always a twinkle in his clear blue eyes. "Come in, come in," he said, radiating the charm that brought him so many friends. "It's a rare day when I can do something for you."

Once seated in his well-appointed living room she asked if he'd heard of Georges Verlag.

"Oh, yes," he said, "one of Zale's men."

She smiled. "So you *do* still have connections—as I hoped."

He said dryly, "My two experiences in prison invoked a great deal of interest among my fellow inmates, and I have never lost an opportunity to broaden my education. It was very educational for me to make friends with them. When I left it was with many well-wishers, who remain in touch. What about Georges Verlag?"

She described her experience in the subway, the attaché case tossed to her, his subsequent departure with the man following him.

"Can you describe the man following him?"

She said efficiently, "Sharp pointed nose, sharp pointed chin, thin lips, roughly six feet tall."

He thought for a few minutes, frowning. "That sounds rather like the young man they call Frankie the Ferret, an unsavory chap, works out of Jake Bodley's group."

"What I want to know," she said firmly, "is whether the

man caught up with Georges and is holding him, or whether Georges escaped him and is in hiding. I want to know if he's alive."

Amos said slyly, "Of course I'd rather know if you've kept the diamonds."

She laughed. "Oh no, they're quite unreachable, the police have them. But my problem is that when I met Georges my name wasn't Karitska, so he has no way to find me—or his diamonds—which worries me."

"I see. . . . Of course eventually the company would contact both police and FBI."

She nodded. "And the police will return the case of diamonds but not to Georges Verlag."

"You are fond of this man?"

"Fond? I scarcely knew him," she said. "He was my husband's friend, they worked for the same firm, but he dined with us several times; it was a decade ago but I have a memory for faces."

"Apparently he does, too," pointed out Amos with humor. "I would not have cared to face you in any police lineup."

She smiled. "You're not thinking of returning to your former . . . does one say 'profession'?"

"Only through my books," he assured her, "although I must say, most of the criminals I write about seem to me depressingly indelicate and clumsy. It will take time, you know, to learn what happened to your subway chap."

"I understand, but you will—"

"I will," he assured her gravely, and Madame Karitska left, feeling that she had done what she could for poor Georges.

At half past three that afternoon she opened her door to her last appointment of the day and was confronted by a fashionably dressed woman who looked both nervous and embarrassed, perhaps never having visited, or expected to visit, either Eighth Street or a clairvoyant, her face a pale oval, skin flawless, eyes carefully made up with eye shadow. Definitely she belonged to Cavendish Square; she looked expensive.

She said, "Karitska? Readings?"

"Yes, do come in," Madame Karitska said cordially.

"I told the cabdriver to wait; it won't take long, will it?"

Madame Karitska smiled. "This is not precisely like a dental appointment. We shall see, shall we?"

"Yes—yes, of course."

The woman followed her inside, looking around in surprise at the sunny book-lined room. "I'd rather not give you my last name, but . . . well, my first name's Anna." She sat down on the edge of the couch as if ready to flee at any minute. "I didn't know what to expect—it's very private. *Very* private." She looked at Madame Karitska with suspicion. "My hairdresser told me about you. I didn't know where else to go. Are you discreet? I hope we don't know the same people."

Madame Karitska wanted to laugh but only waved her hand gracefully at her small living room. She knew a number of people on Cavendish Square, had been there, after all, only two hours ago, but she saw no purpose in saying so. "Unless you frequent Eighth Street I really doubt that we'll meet again."

"You see," she said, "it's about my husband."

Madame Karitska sighed; *another erring husband,* she thought; *I must be tired,* and reminded herself that love, money and grief were what usually brought people to her door. Patience was needed; bills had to be paid.

"Have *you* been married?" demanded the woman.

Amused, Madame Karitska said, "Actually three times, yes. Once for survival when I was fifteen, once for love, once for comfort and companionship."

"Oh," the woman said, startled. "I suppose I should apologize for prying—"

"Yes, you should," agreed Madame Karitska calmly, and waited. After all, she did not have to *like* her clients.

"Well, I'm sorry," Anna said peevishly, "but this is embarrassing."

"Yes, but you'd come about your husband?"

She nodded. "We're *very* happily married," she said defiantly, "but I hardly ever see him; he's become so . . . so secretive since he left his *very* important job a year ago. He's a computer expert, you see, and considered a genius. And with two friends—one of them from Intel and one from IBM, the three left to begin their own electronic company—but in *Maine,*" she said with a catch in her voice, "and he refuses my moving there to be with him."

There were tears in her eyes now. "Our home is here in

Trafton, you see, but he comes back so seldom, I scarcely see him at all these days, and . . ." She hesitated and then said at last, "I keep wondering if he's seeing another woman. Up there. In Maine. And my hairdresser said that if I brought you something of his—"

"It's called psychometry," explained Madame Karitska gently. "Any object worn by a person for a length of time acquires vibrations, energy, tone from that person. What have you brought me?"

From her purse she extracted a wristwatch with a frayed leather band. "He wore this until last month, when he finally bought a new one here in Trafton, on one of his few very short visits. He's worn it for years and years."

Handing it to Madame Karitska she finally allowed herself to sit back on the couch, her eyes watching as she waited.

Madame Karitska cupped the watch loosely in both hands and closed her eyes, and almost at once was jolted by the impressions that reached her. She said reluctantly, "His mind— it whirls, never stills. Obsessive. Brilliant, yes, but not restful."

"I told you he's a genius," the woman reminded her.

But something was wrong, very wrong, thought Madame Karitska, as wave after wave of negativeness reached her. There was malice, a sense of destructiveness, a sense almost of madness. It frightened her, and she dropped the wristwatch and opened her eyes. Steadying herself she said, "At least I can tell you firmly there is no other woman."

Anna's eyes brightened. "But then—what is it?"

"His work," said Madame Karitska. "It completely absorbs him. He—they?—something is being invented, something new. It consumes, excites him. There is a feeling of feverish research. Something new . . ." she repeated.

And dangerous, but she did not add this. She returned the watch to the woman, not wanting to hold it a minute longer; it was too unsettling. "The important thing—what troubled you most, of course—is that there is no other woman. Absolutely no woman."

Not even you, she thought, but refrained from saying this. Instead, regarding her with compassion she added, "It would be sensible, would it not, if you found some work of interest to keep you occupied while he is so intensely involved?"

"Work?" She looked shocked. "But I haven't worked in years. I was a model before I married, but I would be too old, surely, for that. Why do you say this?"

"Because," Madame Karitska told her carefully, "for the moment he has committed himself entirely elsewhere, and what better than to cultivate a life of your own?"

"But—"

"Volunteer work, perhaps? All your waking hours center on him, do they not?" Seeing her face turn sullen she made an appeal to her vanity. "Such worry and frustration will *age* you. Add lines to your face."

She was vain enough for this to penetrate. "Age me?" she faltered.

"But enough," said Madame Karitska, rising. "Think about it. Work is always good for the soul."

Reluctantly the woman rose. "I just wish I could know what is so interesting, working in a small town in Maine like Denby." She sighed but gave Madame Karitska a forced smile. "What do you charge?"

"I prefer to let my clients decide that."

The woman reached into her purse, but so clumsily that a shower of memo notes fell out of it to the floor. After bending over to pick them up she placed a fifty-dollar bill on the table. "And you're absolutely sure there's no other woman?"

"Absolutely," Madame Karitska assured her.

"Then I thank you. Marjorie said . . . yes, I will believe you. I must."

And she was gone. The taxi had waited—for a woman of such means a taxi would always wait, reflected Madame Karitska—and noticing a slip of paper on the floor she picked it up. It appeared to be a list for camping: *sleeping bag,* she read, *five kerosene lamps, wood for fireplace, canned goods, water in gallon jugs . . .* It certainly didn't match the woman who had just left, but obviously it had dropped from her purse. She placed it on her bookcase, should the woman miss it and return for it. She glanced at the clock; she had no evening appointments and she had fifty dollars, more than she had expected for this day when added to the amount from her four clients of the morning.

With a decisive nod she pocketed the fifty-dollar bill, locked the door of her apartment, and set out for Sixth Street, a notorious neighborhood for anyone with a fifty-dollar bill, but she had been there before. She was heading for a certain hole-in-the-wall storefront with a sign that read HELP SAVE TOMORROW, and it was necessary to pass hustlers, drug dealers, glares, and a few whistles until she reached the shabby entrance with its peeling sign.

She entered to find Daniel Henry standing over a pile of T-shirts on the counter and sorting them. Over in a corner several small boys were looking over the few books in a bookcase. Glancing up, Daniel grinned his pleasure with a "Madame Karitska!" leaving her to reflect, not without humor, that on this street the "Madame" could easily be misunderstood.

Daniel was big and well-muscled and black; he was an ex-convict, and if she had told him that on the street one day as she passed his store a sense of his personality had caused her to pause, not even seeing him, and had drawn her inside to meet him, he would no doubt have thought her quite mad, when in fact she had never before sensed a man so dedicated to helping rescue the flock of sad, dangerous, and hopeless people he lived among. A local church contributed some money, but never enough.

"I've had a good week, Daniel," she told him, and placed the fifty-dollar bill on his counter.

His mouth dropped open. "Madame Karitska—"

She laughed. "Not again! I've told you, I've many times in my life gone hungry for want of money."

His broad scarred face beamed at her. "Hard to believe."

"Believe!" she said, and as she returned to the door he followed and shouted, "Hey, you guys, let her pass, you hear? She's a *lady*."

With a feeling that Anna's fifty dollars had been well

placed, she strolled back to Eighth Street. The sun had begun its descent behind the taller buildings of the city, and the sky was fading into gray. It had been a surprisingly busy day, and she could look forward now to meditating, to savoring her dinner of *tajine*, and she might listen to Bach, or perhaps tonight she would choose Edith Piaf.

6

Madame Karitska had begun to notice the new family that had moved in across the street from her. The father was seen only rarely, when he returned in his work clothes from whatever job paid for their rent and food. The mother did a great deal of fussing over a pretty little girl about seven years old. There was a boy, too, but little attention seemed to be paid to him; he was younger, perhaps five or six, and the few times that Madame Karitska had seen the three of them go out together in the morning the boy still occupied a stroller, never smiled, and appeared simply to stare straight ahead of him with no expression at all. The girl was vivacious and skipped happily beside her mother, always with a bright ribbon in her dark hair, but she too ignored her brother in the stroller. To Madame Karitska the boy's being conveyed in a stroller at his age seemed odd, and she wondered if perhaps his legs were deformed, but she was accustomed to this automatic awareness of others without allowing it to be more than idle curiosity.

At least until the woman knocked on her door sharply that noon when Madame Karitska was fortunately between clients . . . or had the woman watched the house, she wondered, waiting for someone other than Kristan or herself to leave? She was a small woman with fierce black eyes, wearing a long and dusty black dress under a cardigan with several buttons missing.

She said at once, defiantly, "No *danaro* . . . no money, I cannot pay, you help peoples?"

Obviously she was on the edge of hysteria, or certainly desperate. "Come in," Madame Karitska told her gently. "Tell me what I can do for a neighbor of mine. Forget the money."

"*Sì? Grazie,*" she said in a softer voice, and followed Madame Karitska inside.

Her accent was thick; Madame Karitska insisted on reheating and bringing her a cup of coffee, the woman following her into the kitchen, too distraught to sit and wait in the living room. They were new here, she said, from a small village in Italia, and her son did not *parlare*—talk, she corrected herself, and her husband had taken Luca to *il dottore* at the clinic, who said—and here tears rose to her eyes—"he said Luca is auto-something and should—must be—what is word, put away?"

"Now that is very sad," agreed Madame Karitska, leading her back into the living room and pouring coffee for her. "Please sit down. Was the word he used *autistic* and the other word *institution*?"

She nodded vigorously. "*Per favore,* can you heal? Like *il dottore*? I hear things, you are *simpatica*?"

Knowing very little Italian Madame Karitska guessed that the woman hoped for the impossible, and yet she had seen the child from across the street, so impassive, so stoic and yet strangely attractive, and she admitted to curiosity, as well as to pity for his distraught mother, who cared. She said, "His name is Luca?"

"Sì. Luca Cialini."

Madame Karitska nodded. "I would have to see him," she said, "and see him *here*." She waved a hand at her living room.

The woman poured out words in alarm, from which Madame Karitska deduced that her husband must not know; it would have to be *segreto*.

"Secret?" suggested Madame Karitska.

The woman nodded vigorously. "He say Luca has *male-dire*," and when this met with a blank and questioning response she scowled, searching for a word. At last, "curse," she blurted out.

Madame Karitska said, "Nonsense," and feeling that she had just about exhausted the little Italian she knew, she reached for pencil and paper and drew a clock for her. "*Domani* . . . in morning? Saturday morning?" And she drew two lines in the circle denoting nine o'clock.

The woman brightened. "*Bene*—good," she said with relief. "*Grazie. Grazie mille*," and putting down her cup of coffee she rose, nodding, smiling, and was escorted to the door, so radiant with hope that Madame Karitska winced.

The next morning she waited for the family with some anticipation, but when the door opened across the street only Mrs. Cialini and the boy emerged. The mother struggled with the stroller, placed Luca in it, and carefully wheeled it across the street. "So—no father," murmured Madame Karitska, this man who believed his son cursed, and opened the door to them; the stroller was left in the hall and Mrs. Cialini carried her son inside to the couch, where he sat staring at the books lining the wall, and then at Madame Karitska, still without expression. His face was well formed, framed by a crop of curly black hair, his eyes wide and fringed with long lashes, but there was no hint of curiosity in them, not even when Madame Karitska sat down beside him on the couch and gently reached for one of his hands, a technique that she rarely used but in this case the only one possible, since no toy had accompanied him; there was only himself. It needed time . . . more time than holding an object that he loved, if he possessed any. He certainly showed signs of neglect, and she wondered if he had been abused—as if neglect in itself was not abuse—and it was necessary for her to close her eyes to shield herself from the boy's mother, who sat on the opposite couch, leaning forward with eagerness, and watching closely.

Very slowly impressions surfaced and grew, until abruptly Madame Karitska removed her hand from his, startled. The boy's eyes met hers for a moment and—incredibly—she thought he looked amused.

She said softly, "He lives in a strange world." When the mother opened her mouth to speak, Madame Karitska signed to her to be silent while she regarded the child thoughtfully. After a few minutes she went to the telephone and dialed the number of the Settlement House, where Jan worked on Saturday mornings, and asked to speak with her.

"Marina, what a surprise," said Jan.

"You're busy, I know," she told her, "but I wonder if—this

noon, or after your work ends—you could come and confirm . . . I have a small boy here who has never talked, quite neglected, his name is Luca. I'd like to know what impressions *you* receive psychically."

"Sounds interesting," said Jan.

"I'd guess he's about six years old," continued Madame Karitska. "An Italian family. The mother doesn't speak much English. I don't know about the husband, but it could be difficult."

"Not really," said Jan cheerfully. "You're forgetting that I spent my junior year at college in Italy. I'm not great but I'm good enough to be resident translator at the Settlement House."

"I *had* forgotten," admitted Madame Karitska. "I've one other request. In your children's day school you have what I can only describe as an electric keyboard, a laptop piano the children play music on?"

"You bet. Good idea—it's a rare child who doesn't react to music. So I'll be leaving at noon and come directly," promised Jan, "and hope your mysterious small boy can be there by half past the hour."

"My fervent thanks, Jan," and hanging up the phone Madame Karitska returned to a frightened mother. "It's all right," she told her soothingly. "Your son interests me very much, and I've asked a friend to come and see Luca later today. Please? At—" Again she drew a clock and sketched in the hour with lines.

She was not comforted. "My husband no like, *no.*"

"He must come, too," Madame Karitska told her sternly.

"If he does not come we will cross the street and *make* him come. This is his *son*, is he not?"

"But you tell me nothing, *nothing*."

Madame Karitska smiled. "I say this—*no* institution for Luca."

The woman brightened. "Dear God, a *miracolo?*" and for a moment Madame Karitska feared that she would kiss her hands. To avoid this she helped her lift Luca into his stroller.

"Tell me," she said, "can Luca walk at all? His legs . . ." She pointed to them. "Yes? No?"

His mother looked suddenly mischievous in the glance she gave her, and much younger. "When Mario go," and her voice was conspiratorial, "Luca *passeggiata*." She thought a minute and then, "He take steps." Abruptly her face saddened. "But Mario, I think he want not even—" She broke off and Madame Karitska watched her push the stroller down the steps and across the street. *Not even to live*, thought Madame Karitska. A serious business, and upsetting, and she returned to her kitchen to rescue her spinach quiche from the oven before her next client arrived.

At quarter past twelve Jan's car drew up to the brownstone, and Madame Karitska went out to meet her, considerably cheered by the sight of her. She was currently wearing her pale blond hair long, and it charmingly framed her piquant face; she was also, Madame Karitska noted, carrying the long toy piano board under one arm, and a book in the other.

"My Italian dictionary," she explained, handing the latter to her. "Just in case. What's it all about, Marina?"

"That," she said, "is what I hope we can find out," and led her inside. "The child is without schooling and virtually an invalid, and yet, and yet . . ." Glancing out the window, "They come now, and thank heaven the father is coming, too."

"Not happily," said Jan, looking over her shoulder. "And the child in a stroller? Why doesn't he carry him for her?"

"Apparently," said Madame Karitska, "he doesn't care to even touch him." He did indeed look furious, his wife submissive but yearning, the boy as passive as usual. Jan at once went out to help pull the stroller up the steps, and the three of them entered, the father grudgingly.

"I not like this, my wife make trouble for us," he said, his English superior to hers. "The boy is not good in the head, he is nothing. *Malo.* Evil."

"This is Jan," said Madame Karitska calmly, "and your wife is very upset about sending Luca away; surely you know this?"

He shrugged. "A man needs a son who will work one day, can walk, talk, earn his living. He is *diverso.* Different. She will not listen."

Madame Karitska gave him a curt glance and told them to sit down, and with a nod to Jan she went into the kitchen to bring out a pot of coffee. When she returned, Jan was holding the child's hand and smiling at him and he was staring at her without expression. To prevent the parents from speaking she gave them each a slice of cake and a cup of coffee, and sat down to watch.

Jan's face was showing a growing astonishment. "It's like . . . like . . ." and to his parents, "You say he never talks, but does he make sounds?"

His mother shrugged. "He will sometimes . . ." She struggled for a word. "Like a bumblebee?"

Jan nodded, and walked over to the keyboard that she'd already plugged into an electrical outlet, and placed it on the child's lap. Grasping one of his fingers she pressed it to a key, and at the sound of the musical note the change was astonishing. A sense of blissful wonder swept over his face; he moved his finger to the next key and then to the next; a little melody developed and then a second finger joined the first to make a chord, and his face was pure delight. Kneeling beside the boy Jan lifted her gaze to his parents and said, "He has been making music in his head—in his *head*, silently, and it's . . . it's . . ."

The father made a face. "So? What is that mean, he is *pazzo*—crazy?"

"No," Madame Karitska told him, "gifted." And to Jan, "When I got through to him this morning he was singing every word of John Painter's 'Once in Old Atlantis.' Silently." And to the mother, "You have a radio?"

"*Sì—sì.*"

Jan said dryly, "I can top that, Marina, he paid no attention to me, he was busy constructing what I swear were chords from Beethoven's Fifth Symphony. Near the end of it, when it rises higher and higher, a part I love." Placing the child's hands on the keyboard again, "Can you say the word *music?*"

The boy looked at his father in terror, but Jan pressed his finger harder. "*Music.*"

His lips contorted, moved, and with effort he said, "Mooick."

There was silence until his father said angrily, "What is this you do? Look at him," he said accusingly, "he is cursed, I tell you. Evil. Rosetta said any son of mine—" He burst into Italian, passionately waving his hands, the only understandable word *Rosetta*, recurring over and over, while Jan looked more and more shocked.

"My God," she murmured, and when he faltered she said, "Rosetta Dellaripa . . . in the small mountain town where they lived she was a *strega*—a witch."

He nodded. "She put a curse on my first son, *sì.*"

Madame Karitska said nothing; she felt a little sick as Jan demanded more from him.

"He says," resumed Jan, "that when Luca was born he was terrified the child would bring them every possible misfortune. He has expected every day the curse on Luca will hurt him, his wife, his daughter, he cannot bear to look at Luca or touch him."

"And why," asked Madame Karitska, "did this horrible woman put this so-called curse on him?"

This needed time, but at last Jan said indignantly, "This wretched Rosetta wanted Luca's father to marry *her* daughter, who had no dowry." With a nod to Luca's mother she added, "*She* had a dowry, he quickly married her and spent her dowry to come to America, and for this Rosetta cursed him, with some sort of frightening ceremony. Sons are important— vital—what better to curse?"

Madame Karitska slowly rose from the couch where she was sitting and walked over to Luca's father and placed a hand on each side of his face, turning it up to her. She said coldly, "You understand enough English to hear what I am going to say. Luca is not cursed; it is *you* who have been cursed. *You.* Denied a son. Too afraid to love him. Too afraid to touch him. You have made your house cold as ice; do you not realize he feels this?" To Jan she said, "Is there a word for *paralyze?*"

Jan reached for her Italian dictionary and thumbed through it. "*Paralizzare?*"

"Exactly," said Madame Karitska. "He feels your hate; he is paralyzed by it. He retreats. You want a son who works, earns money, walks, talks? This Luca of yours may, with care, grow up to make more money than you will ever see. He is gifted. Bright. Like the sun."

He stared at her, stupefied.

To Mrs. Cialini she said, "Bring Luca to him."

Timidly she picked up Luca and carried him to his father, "Hold him. *Hold* him. There is no Rosetta here, you are in America. *Hold* him," Madame Karitska told him.

He did not reach out his arms, but he allowed Luca to be placed in his lap. For a moment panic appeared to overwhelm him, and then he looked down at Luca and, feeling the weight of him sliding, grasped him closer. He stared down at Luca and Luca looked up at him and they appeared to examine each other, until with dignity Mario said to his wife, "We go home now, Maria."

His wife moved toward the stroller but he shook his head. "Me, I carry him, Maria."

Without a word, or a nod to Madame Karitska or Jan, he walked out of the room, his wife behind him.

"A man of pride," murmured Madame Karitska dryly.

"Too macho to accept the scoldings of two mere women," laughed Jan. "We run into this occasionally at the Settlement House with immigrant families who come from male-oriented societies."

Madame Karitska nodded. "I accept the rudeness, but what now for Luca?"

"Leave it to me," said Jan. "You've planted real doubts in that man about the curse. I'd like Lou Devoe to see Luca—our part-time child psychologist. She won't charge and I'll see to it that someone drives him to her office and returns him—he'll love the toys there. He needs school, of course, but not until he's freed of his fears to talk, and Trafton has two special schools for the unusually gifted."

"And then?"

"Why, our dear Mr. Faber-Jones," she said with a smile.

"Jan," protested Madame Karitska, "we can't keep asking him to subsidize waifs."

"*Waifs!*" exclaimed Jan. "You call John Painter a waif? The story I heard is that you rescued John Painter just as he was about to be arrested for shoplifting, heard the song he'd written, and insisted Faber-Jones come at once to hear it, and then to start Pisces Record Company to record 'Once in Old Atlantis,' a song that's made Faber-Jones even richer, and John Painter rich, too. He owes you, Marina."

Madame Karitska winced. "I feel no debt—except to the child Luca."

Jan patted her on the arm. "Don't worry, it's far too early to ask his help." With a glance at her watch she said, "I've got to rush off now, I've a date with a detective lieutenant whom I dearly love and who has the afternoon off. Call me anytime, Marina," and with a grin she added, "*Ciao*, Marina!" and was gone.

Once she was alone Madame Karitska smiled at Jan's reminding her of John Painter. A very satisfying experience that had been, she thought, and after a few minutes she walked across the room to her cassette player, sorted through the symphonies to reach a certain song, and, as she flicked on the sound, John Painter's voice filled the living room.

Once in old Atlantis,
I loved a lady pure . . .
And then the waters rose
And death was black and cold.
Once in Indian days
I loved a maiden pure . . .
But white men shot her through the heart
And I was left to grieve.
I saw her once in Auschwitz
Young, dressed all in black . . .
Our eyes met once beside the wall—
The Nazis shot her dead.
She's gone, I cannot find her,
A fortune-teller says "Not yet,"
For life's a slowly turning wheel
And this turn's not for love . . .

His voice and the guitar faded away until, with a dramatic sweep of his fingers across its strings he repeated, "And this turn's not for love," and abruptly the music ended.

Yes, she thought, nodding, she really must approach Faber-Jones soon about Luca, who might, in time, become an equal surprise for him.

7

It was several days later when Madame Karitska found Betsy Oliver lurking in her hallway, too shy to knock and apparently not daring to make an appointment that she couldn't afford. She turned scarlet when she was found, and stammered an apology. "You said," she began, "I mean you told me—and you're the only one who liked my sketches, and—"

"And I told you I hoped that you'd come back in a week or so to see your sketch framed and hung, yes."

"You don't mind?" she said eagerly. "Are you busy?"

"My dear, you were *invited*. And I'm free for an hour and do come in. You'll find your sketch on the wall over there," she told her, pointing. "What's more, there's someone I'd like you to meet."

She left Betsy standing in front of the casual sketch of her daughter, which looked astonishingly uncasual and professional, now that it was matted and framed. Going to the telephone she was relieved to find that Kristan was at work upstairs in his studio. She said, "The young woman whose work I showed you some days ago is here, Kristan. Would you have a few minutes to give counsel? Could I send her up to you?"

Kristan, always ironic, said, "My snakes would doubtless terrify her. I need a break; I'll come down."

In a few minutes he noisily thundered down the stairs and walked in, his beard daubed with scarlet today, and giving Betsy a keen glance he said, "So."

Both of them tried to avoid looking at the bruise on Betsy's cheek.

"This," Madame Karitska told her, "is Kristan Seversky, who works upstairs and is a professional artist, and I showed him your sketch. Now do sit down while I fetch some coffee for you."

"I shall be very stern," Kristan told the girl. "You've drawn only faces?"

Betsy nodded, regarding him with awe.

"No figures yet?"

She shook her head.

"Have you done any work in colors?"

"I don't have any," she admitted.

"You will need training," he said. "Classes in life—nudes—figures, but—"

"But?" asked Madame Karitska, bringing in coffee and placing the carafe on the table with three cups. "But what, Kristan?"

"But to earn money to live on now—and for further training . . ." He got up and removed the framed sketch from the wall. "You have more of these?"

"Yes," said Betsy.

"Good. You're willing to start small?"

"Small?" she echoed, confused.

"I have connections with two greeting card companies here in Trafton, and although it is only summer they begin already to plan for Christmas, and they've a penchant for angels. I would say that one of these companies would be seized with delight at such luminous faces, possibly both of them. They do not pay extremely well, but enough to keep bread on your table, and enough for you take a class when you can afford it, to see if you can draw bodies as well, and to support extending your talent. Here," he said, and reached into a paper bag he'd brought with him, and from it drew out a hand-carved, jointed figure of a man. "With this you can practice. You see the joints? His figure stands. He sits, and you can sketch him seated. You move arms and legs and sketch him running. With this you can practice how the human figure moves."

"You mean—" began Betsy in surprise.

"Yes, I lend it to you."

Betsy stared at him with wide eyes. "But this is so . . . so very *kind* of you."

"I am not kind," he said brusquely. "I am only an artist who appreciates. Now I want you to go home, gather up all the sketches you have made, and take them to each of these companies downtown. I have written their names down for you here, and the names of the man or woman you must see, and when you are ready to visit them, here is my phone number; I will call and tell them you're coming."

Betsy looked overwhelmed and a little frightened, and his voice turned kinder. He said gravely, "I can assure you that if they are in their right minds, one of them will surely be eager to use your work; if not, there is still New York. In the meantime I say to you that your drawings are wonderfully original and fresh."

"You, too?" she marveled. "Madame Karitska said—but I didn't dare—how can I *ever* thank—"

He cut her off, looking pained. "I return now to my painting," he announced, and to Madame Karitska with a suddenly teasing, boyish smile, "To my snakes."

With a nod he opened the door and walked out, closing it behind him.

When he was gone Betsy looked at Madame Karitska with a sense of wonder. She said, "I want you to know that I never expected *help*, or anything like this. I came back for . . . for comfort, I guess. To tell you I refused to go with Arthur— Alpha, I mean—and there was no one else to tell. I just knew I couldn't let Alice—our daughter—go to that place, the Guardian place." Her hand moved to the bruise on her cheek.

"He hit you."

Betsy nodded. "He left two days ago. He was furious. It's taken so much out of me, I've felt so shaken and lost—"

"Then I'm glad you came."

"But now—I was going to look for a waitress job," she said, and suddenly smiled; her smile was radiant. "Now I have something to go home for, something to do. How can I ever thank you and Mr. Seversky?"

Madame Karitska said lightly, "There are some who say

there are no accidents in life, and it may be that we were meant to meet." With a glance at her watch, "Now you must go home and collect your sketches—I assume you've done more since I saw you—and look to your future, not your past."

"Oh I will, I will," promised Betsy.

Madame Karitska lifted the framed sketch from her wall. "Take this with you—on loan—because the frame shows it off so well, it enhances it, and there should be no need for you to frame the others." *Or the money to frame them*, she thought, but did not say.

Betsy gathered up the jointed wooden figure—"this will be wonderful to work with"—and proudly added the framed sketch. "You must have appointments, so I'll go, but—" She leaned over and kissed Madame Karitska on the cheek. "But suddenly there's so much to do—and without hiding it from my husband!"

8

Madame Karitska did not often have male clients, and she quite understood that masculine pride was usually involved. She was therefore pleased when a Mr. Jason Hendricks made an appointment, but less pleased when he arrived: the poor man looked pale and emaciated, with a haunted look in his eyes, and she found herself hoping that he did not assume she was a healer of sorts, for he looked very ill.

His first words to her were, "I've gone to every doctor possible," and she flinched. "I don't have AIDS, I don't have tuberculosis, or parasites or ulcers, I've been tested and tested and tested."

As gently as possible she told him that she did not deal in alternative medicines—*or miracles*, she wanted to say, but didn't.

"I don't expect that," he told her coldly. "And I don't know why I'm here. A neighbor said I could at least keep trying."

She nodded. "An act of desperation—I quite understand."

"Do you?" he demanded. "Do you?"

"Life has many desperate chapters," she told him, and looking at him more closely she realized that not long ago he must have been a handsome man, and certainly younger than he looked now. "Perhaps over a cup of green tea we can talk better," she told him, and went into the kitchen to brew it.

When she returned he was looking over the books in her bookcase with interest. "I see that you have several interesting books on Afghanistan. Have you traveled there?"

She smiled. "My family lived in Kabul for a few years when I was a child. Not entirely by choice; we were refugees and very poor. Do you know the country?"

"Only briefly, as a travel writer, before the Taliban took over." With relief he lowered himself to the couch and watched her pour him a cup of tea. He said carefully, "You understand I expect nothing from you, but this woman I scarcely know—a neighbor—told me about you, and that possibly—well, frankly," he added, "I was entertaining the thought of ending my life, which has pretty much happened already." He added dryly, "But without the last rites. She said you saw things?" With a forced smile and a shaking hand he lifted the cup of tea to his lips, and then put it down before it spilled.

"Have you eaten lately?" she asked.

He shrugged. "Nothing solid. No appetite."

"Sleep?"

"Only with dread, and nightmares," and quickly changing the subject, "She said I should bring with me something I've worn for years?"

Madame Karitska nodded. "Yes, and have you?"

"My wallet," he said, and fumbled in his jacket pocket for a worn and shabby wallet. "It's gone everywhere with me for years." He gave a feeble laugh. "I grow notoriously attached to things, no matter how old, perhaps because I move around so much in my travels."

She smiled. "I know that feeling . . . old clothes, old friends, old books. One needs constants in a traveling life."

He seemed to suddenly see her more clearly now. "As a refugee you really would know that, wouldn't you."

She nodded. "Oh yes. When I was a child I once found a milk white stone, almost translucent; I thought it more beautiful than any jewel—we had no toys—and fortunately it was small enough to carry in my pocket; I cherished it for years."

He nodded. "That I can understand. I often find the oddest souvenirs to bring back with me, never touristy, but satisfying for some inexplicable reason." He reached across the table and gave his wallet to her. "It's all yours."

"Thank you. Now if you will be very still, it's called psychometry, and I must deeply concentrate on what it tells me." *If the gods are smiling,* she added to herself. "And if you've had many experiences as a traveler there will be many impressions. This may take some time, so please relax."

Holding the wallet cupped in her hands she closed her eyes and this time added a brief prayer. With concentration, impressions began to surface . . . a restless, intelligent man . . . well traveled, hungry for knowledge . . . curious and talented . . . a woman in a sari whom he'd loved . . . desert sands and— She was suddenly startled enough to open her eyes. Admitting less than she received she said, "But I have to tell you at once the impressions I receive are very strong. What you suffer from no doctor here can help, and no prescription cure."

Dismayed and shocked he said, "Good God, what is it?"

She said softly, "A sickness of the spirit. Of the soul."

"The soul?" he blurted out. "But that's—"

"Ridiculous? You do have a soul," she reminded him.

"Of course, but—"

"Please . . . let me clear up one possibility first. You've not had any extremely traumatic experience lately? Depression, loss, for instance?"

He said bitterly, "Both of those since I've begun—at the age of thirty-six—to feel a hundred years old with this illness, yes. Loss? My health. Depression? I can no longer *work*."

She nodded. "And you returned from your travels how long ago?"

"Two and a half months ago."

"And began feeling ill on your return?"

"Actually on the plane home, it was a long flight."

She said abruptly, "Did you drive here?"

"Is that all you can say?" he demanded. "No, I didn't feel well enough to drive here, I took a taxi."

"Too weak," she said, nodding. "I'm going to call a taxi now for us."

"Look here," he protested, "I came here—"

"To be helped," she told him. "We now go to a friend of mine for advice."

He said accusingly, "I begin to think you a bloody quack."

She turned at the telephone and smiled. "I've been called worse, Mr. Hendricks. What I gave you was a diagnosis, now we must find the cure."

"Then you're keeping something from me. Am I going to die?"

But she was already ordering a cab, and he waited in an angry silence.

"We will wait outside," she told him, "there will be a taxi in four minutes."

He was even more outraged when the cab drove them only two blocks down to Sixth Street, turned to the right and passed groups of idle young men and boys who looked extremely intimidating, but apparently not to his companion. The cab stopped at a storefront with the sign HELP SAVE TO-MORROW. "Please wait," she told the driver.

With resentment Mr. Hendricks climbed out and followed her into a narrow shop full of cartons of shoes and old clothes hanging on rods, its only occupant a huge black man who appeared to be in charge. He said with a warm smile, "Welcome, Madame Karitska!" and then looked doubtfully at her companion.

"Daniel," she said, "this is Mr. Hendricks, a travel writer who two and a half months ago returned from Africa, much healthier than he is now."

Hendricks turned to stare at her. "But I didn't tell you I'd been in Africa!"

"No," she said, "you didn't have to."

Daniel looked at Hendricks and whistled through his teeth. "He has the look of death on him, that's for sure."

She nodded. "And has been tested for every possible tropical disease. You once spoke of a doctor who attends the church that contributes to your store. . . ."

Daniel slowly nodded. "Yes, Dr. Idowi. You really think—"

"It's what I saw, Daniel," she said softly. "Very clearly."

Daniel nodded. "If you give me a quarter to make the phone call—the pay phone's just down the street."

Hendricks, clearly worried, said, "What *is* it you saw? For God's sake tell me."

But Daniel was already returning. "I tell him good, Madame Karitska. He is very, very interested. Just back from university lecture and has one hour before patients now. You go, he is in his office." He wrote down the address on a scrap of paper.

They returned to the taxi, whose driver had begun to look anxious, considering the neighborhood, and Madame Karitska gave him the address on Tenth Street.

"Oh, the clinic," said the driver with relief, nodding, and soon deposited them in front of a large brick building bearing a directory of doctors below its sign.

It was refreshingly cool inside; they took the elevator up to the third floor, and when they entered room 305, Hendricks visibly relaxed at the sight of a perfectly normal reception room with a nurse. The nurse, her face a strikingly dark contrast to her starched white uniform, told them the doctor was waiting for them, and opened the door to his office.

Dr. Idowi was a man in midlife, a tall African American with a fringe of gray beard lining a strong jaw, and bright, intelligent eyes. He rose to shake hands with them and then pointed to the two chairs near his desk. "Please be seated," he said, giving Hendricks a keen glance, and Madame Karitska a smile. "I have heard of you from Daniel, who has spoken to me about you," he told her. Gravely he added, "And you saw what?"

"A sickness of the soul."

With a nod he turned to Hendricks. "And you have been tested for bilharzia, yellow fever, cholera, hepatitis, polio, meningitis, and parasites?"

Hendricks nodded. "Everything."

Leaning back in his chair he said, "Tell me about your visit to Africa, Mr. Hendricks, your itinerary and what particularly interested you."

Hendricks shrugged. "If it's important I don't mind. I intended to visit the sub-Sahara, but first I stopped briefly—or so I thought—in Kenya, to say hello to a friend of mine, Colin Birchwood, in the Peace Corps. We were in college together, roommates. . . . He met my plane, he and a young African aide and friend named Funtua. And what Colin told me about their work in the bush, in a village in the interior, so interested me I decided to stay . . . to go back with them to their village and spend a few weeks gathering material there, for a book or at least an article."

"Go on," said the doctor.

Hendricks's voice became eager as he continued. "I've always been intensely interested in belief systems, especially native religions, and here was my chance to learn firsthand of what I'd only read about. I mean, they really do live with the spirits of their ancestors, offer gifts to them to honor or placate them ... such rich material! And then their spirit healers ..."

"I am not unfamiliar with them," commented Dr. Idowi dryly. "Pray go on."

"Colin, my Peace Corps friend, told me of an American doctor who had been there for years, quite revolutionary—at least he would be here in America, I guess—because he'd become interested in the natives' traditional medicine and he felt strongly that it should be combined with our modern medicine. Colin and Funtua took me to meet him, and I actually went with the doctor—and Colin and Funtua—to interview, through him, a diviner, and later we witnessed a healing by a native who communicated, apparently, with antagonistic spirits. I've got notes on all this. I believe the good spirits are called Rohanis, the very bad spirits Shetanis."

"Black magic, white magic," murmured Dr. Idowi.

Hendricks nodded. "In America they'd call it witchcraft, I suppose? At least the government there tries to suppress *actual* witchcraft, but this seemed straightforward, all of it. I mean, Colin had experienced terrible headaches—migraines—at one time, and Funtua, whose father was a healer, gave him herbs that had cured him, and he and Funtua—"

Dr. Idowi nodded. "They worked together? Had a close relationship?"

"Oh, very," Hendricks said. "Colin called him his brother, and Funtua beamed and said yes, they were brothers."

Amused, Dr. Idowi said, "And did Funtua adopt you, too?"

Hendricks smiled. "As a cousin, at least. He was fascinated, listened wide-eyed to Colin and me talking about our college days, and when Funtua didn't understand a word Colin translated it in Swahili—or maybe Hausa, since Funtua was a member of the Chaamba tribe. He spoke English well but didn't understand American slang, which needed explaining."

"Chaamba," mused Dr. Idowi. "And have you brought souvenirs back with you?"

Hendricks shrugged. "A few wood carvings, and a necklace of charms." He reached inside his shirt and brought out a thin leather cord from which hung a tiny cloth bag. "Funtua called them gris-gris," he said. "The charms."

"Yes, I know," Dr. Idowi said dryly. "It is a Hausa word, and the Chaamba speak Hausa. Until I was nine years old I lived in a village in Africa and am well acquainted with gris-gris. Do you mind if I cut this open just to see what's in it?"

"Not if it helps," said Hendricks. "But you can't possibly think, if you're talking spirits and sorcery, that anything could reach thousands of miles to affect me!"

Without replying Dr. Idowi produced a penknife and slit open the tiny sack. "Feathers," he murmured. "These slips of paper are no doubt verses from the Koran . . . a stone . . . and these crumbled shreds of—of *wood*, yes—look like scrapings from the bark of a tree or shrub." He frowned. "I don't know what they would be." He reached into his desk and brought out a magnifying glass.

"*Damn*," said Hendricks suddenly, and they looked at him in surprise. "I can tell you what they're for; how could I have forgotten? They're what cured Colin of migraine headaches. Headaches, nightmares—my God, the headaches I've had! I could have cured myself of *them*, if I'd remembered."

Dr. Idowi nodded. "Yes, but I'd like to have this analyzed in my lab, since you're consulting me." He frowned. "I would also like to see the wood carvings you returned with."

"Look here," Hendricks said, "are you suggesting voodoo of some sort?"

"Voodoo," said Dr. Idowi coolly, "is a religion of the Caribbean. It's true that elements of it from Africa have been incorporated into it—but also corrupted," he added distastefully. "We are dealing with Africa now, not the Caribbean." With a glance at his watch he said, "My next patient is due shortly, but I ask two things of you. I want you to return tomorrow at two o'clock, and I think it might be of interest to Madame Karitska—and perhaps useful—to return with you, since it was she who . . . If you have the time?"

Madame Karitska nodded. "I'll make time."

"But as for you, Mr. Hendricks," he said, "I wish you to deliver to me *today*, this afternoon, the wood carvings—all of them—that you brought back with you from Africa. If I am occupied, please leave them with my nurse."

"Oh for heaven's sake," grumbled Hendricks.

"Yes," smiled Dr. Idowi, "for heaven's sake."

Madame Karitska had two clients the next morning, but between their arrivals and departures her thoughts returned to Jason Hendricks. If she could acknowledge that her gift of clairvoyance was a mystery, she was not as skeptical as Hendricks about anything equally as strange as his illness. There were dimensions to life that even physicists conceded were undiscovered as yet; the mind was a powerful instrument, given to depressions and illusions, hopes, desires and suggestion. It was like a half-empty room, ready in children to be filled with optimism or pessimism, tricks of thought, despair, joy, rejection, love, buried memories that could be triggered by an aroma, a voice, a word ill-spoken, a mood, a dream. She found herself intensely curious as to what Dr. Idowi might find, and what would happen to Jason Hendricks if he found nothing to help him.

At a few minutes after two o'clock that afternoon she and Mr. Hendricks were ushered by the nurse into Dr. Idowi's office. He had a pleasant hello for them and bade them be seated, and after giving each of them a thoughtful glance he reached down and brought up a basket from beside his desk. To Madame Karitska he explained, "These are the wood carvings Mr. Hendricks brought to me yesterday."

To Hendricks he said, bringing them out of the basket one by one, "Several of these are very handsome, especially the masks. I congratulate you on your taste and acumen."

Hendricks said, "Harmless, then? I don't know whether to feel relieved or discouraged. I'd begun to think, overnight, that you might find a clue to this horrible wasting away, which is what it feels like."

"On the contrary," said Dr. Idowi, "may I ask if by chance you had a mustache when you were in Kenya?"

"Mustache!" He gave a derisive laugh. "Yes, briefly. Less shaving, less nuisance."

"Then we have this," said Dr. Idowi, and brought out the

primitive carving of a man, roughly eight inches in height, its body very short, its head large. "Madame Karitska?" he said.

She leaned closer to look at the disproportionate head and then glanced at Hendricks, frowning. "The same shape of the head as his, but those tufts of what—grass?—attached under the nose, are they supposed to be a mustache?"

"Yes . . . Tell me, Mr. Hendricks, have you kept this carving near you where you live?"

"Near me? Well, yes, on the lamp table next my bed."

Dr. Idowi turned the carving sideways. "You notice the large convoluted ears?"

Hendricks laughed. "My ears—if that's what you're implying—certainly aren't that large. What's the matter with them?"

Dr. Idowi sighed. "I have to tell you, Mr. Hendricks, that when witch doctors make an effigy of a person whom they want to die, they place Abrus seeds in their ears." With a tweezer he brought out a small, hard red seed. "This is an Abrus seed. There is also one in the other ear."

Hendricks stammered, "That's ridiculous; I met no one who wanted to kill me."

"African natives wear no mustaches, Mr. Hendricks."

"I tell you, there couldn't be anyone—"

"Then consider this," continued Dr. Idowi, shaking out the shreds of bark from an envelope. "The lab has analyzed these scrapings that were given you for headaches."

"Yes—I only wish I'd thought to use it."

"Lucky for you that you didn't or you'd be dead," he said

calmly. "The lab analyzed this. They couldn't identify what it came from, it being foreign to them, but its substance was only too familiar to them; they diagnosed its toxic substance as a digitalis-like glyoside. I suspect it came from the Mukoso tree. . . . If it was placed in a glass of water, wine or beer, and you drank it you'd be dead very, *very* quickly. I think," he said gently, "that you somehow met with a *very* bad spirit."

Hendricks, gaping at him in shock, said, "But who?"

"Perhaps—from what I hear of Madame Karitska's talents, she can tell us. There is first of all the carving, the effigy of you, Mr. Hendricks, and someone very powerful carved it, hoping for a slow death for you, and if that failed, if you were only sick and turned to the medicine that was supposed to be for headaches, but are the roots of what would be Mukoso in Kenya, this would have done the trick and finished you off neatly and forever." He handed the carving to Madame Karitska. "Can you tell us who did this?"

Reluctantly she accepted the effigy and held it, closing her eyes. For a moment there was silence and then she said, "Each stroke of the knife that carved this was done with a terrible hatred and—yes, jealousy. Insane jealousy. A young man, I feel."

"White or black?" inquired Dr. Idowi.

"Black," she said, and shivered. "Take it away, *please*."

Dr. Idowi nodded. "Funtua, I would suspect. You canceled your sub-Sahara trip, Mr. Hendricks, but ironically met with a member of the Chaamba tribe from the sub-Sahara, and you mentioned that Funtua was a Chaamba. This is a tribe known for the power of the spells they cast—love potions, yes, and amulets, but also for the very powerful spells they are able to cast on victims *both near and far away*."

This met with a stunned silence. "But he was so *friendly*," protested Hendricks.

Dr. Idowi nodded. "And I would guess very jealous of your relationship with Colin, as you spoke of old times together. He had to share you with his hero, his mentor, his friend— perhaps his only friend—and he felt abandoned, left out. Hate is very much a component of jealousy. And you say you slept each night with this beside you?"

Hendricks said, "But you really think—so many continents away?"

"I think yes," the doctor told him gravely. "It's been known to happen. The test will lie in what happens to you when this effigy is removed from your presence. This carving has to be destroyed; I'll have to do some research on that, it's a danger- ous process, I suspect, but in the meantime it stays here, Mr. Hendricks, for me to deal with, and I suggest you begin a cleansing of your body. . . ."

"How?"

"Acupuncture, perhaps . . . A reliable herbalist. Vitamins . . . But I believe you will begin to heal, I really do."

Hendricks drew a deep sigh. "I will pray for that."

Dr. Idowi smiled faintly. "Prayer helps too, my friend. My nurse will send my bill if you leave your address with her, but I'll charge you only for the lab work." To Madame Karitska he said, "You have brought me a very interesting case, but I shall hope you bring me no more."

"Granted," she told him, and rose to shake hands with him.

It was three weeks later, when Madame Karitska was eating her breakfast, that she heard a knock on her door. "It's open," she called, thinking it was Kristan, but it was Jason Hendricks who entered. A very different Jason Hendricks, and she rose from her chair in surprise. He stood by the door beaming at her, his face a normal color, his stance erect, his eyes bright with the boyish look of someone bringing a gift—and it *was* a gift, seeing him look younger and healthy again.

He said, "I forgot to pay you. I had to come and show you how I am now, but to think I walked away, so skeptical and ill, that I didn't remember to pay you!"

"I quite understood," she assured him gravely.

"I've just left one hundred dollars with Daniel," he told her, "and an armful of books for his store, and for you . . ." From behind him he brought out a bouquet of red roses. "My payment's in the envelope tucked inside the roses. It could never be enough, though, when what I owe you is my life." He hesitated and then abruptly sat down on the edge of her couch.

"I didn't know what to do about my friend Colin in the Peace Corps," he told her, frowning.

She nodded, waiting.

"I felt he ought to know. I mean, if circumstances changed, Colin could be in danger, too."

"You wrote him?"

He shook his head. "I had the awful feeling my letter might be intercepted by Funtua. I telephoned the District Officer in the nearest town and asked him to send a message to Colin to come to this town and phone me collect." He added wryly, "I gave only my phone number, not my name, and said it was a family emergency. Which," he added, "is how paranoid I've grown."

She smiled. "On the whole, I think that very sensible. You've heard from Colin?"

Hendricks nodded. "It was several days before he was able to leave the village and call me, and it cost a small fortune convincing him about the poison and the effigy. He admitted that Funtua could be what he called 'tiresomely possessive' at times, but he had no idea—I mean, he found it hard to believe what I'd gone through. He was alarmed enough to think of leaving at once, quickly, secretly. Afraid Funtua might guess what he'd learned. But then—"

"But then?" asked Madame Karitska.

"Then he realized he'd have to return to the village for his passport and money, and he decided that he'd tell Funtua he must go back to the States on a family matter, a funeral." He hesitated, frowning. "I reminded him—told him—that Funtua might not like that, might not like that at *all*, and to be careful, very careful what he ate and drank before he left."

He was silent and then he added in a troubled voice, "I just hope he got away in time."

9

It was the next morning when her good friend Mr. Faber-Jones knocked at her door. "Is this a bad time for you?" he asked anxiously. "I should have telephoned first, but—"

"But something has happened," she said, nodding. "You know I'm always delighted to see you, and I've no appointment until nine o'clock."

It still amused her that this small, plump, middle-aged man, so impeccably dressed and wealthy, had suddenly discovered in midlife—and very much against his will —that he had become psychic. She had met him only a few weeks after she'd hung her sign in the window, and with no money to pay her next month's rent she'd reluctantly agreed to replace a fortune-teller at a charity party on Cavendish Square, given by a Mrs. Faber-Jones. Once placed under a tent in the garden she'd been intrigued about the questions asked of her by an onlooker, and she in turn had questioned him.

He was Mr. Faber-Jones, he'd said, and miserably he admitted that a few months ago, on leaving his office in the Pratt Building, he'd had a very bad fall on the ice and had

been taken unconscious to the hospital, and when he'd finally
regained consiousness . . .

But she had already guessed what upset him and nodded.
"The blow to your head had changed you."

"The things I *saw!*" He'd groaned, and she had looked at
this conventional businessman with interest. After attempt-
ing to comfort him over a period of weeks, she had suggested
that he use this gift of clairvoyance that had so astonishingly
overtaken him in midlife. There had been evenings when he
and young Gavin O'Connell, still a student at Saint Bonaven-
ture's, had come to her apartment to help him practice concentration and how to direct it, but he had refused to be
called anything but Faber-Jones, which had mystified them
until at last he confided that his first name was Polonius.
Faber-Jones he had remained.

Now he dropped to her couch and said nervously, "You've
not forgotten my dinner party Sunday night?"

"Of course not," she told him, "I'm bringing baklava,
remember?"

"Oh yes," he said, and sighed. "And there'll be one guest
you'll find interesting, ex-CIA, ex–State Department, I've
known him for years."

"My friend," she said gently, "what *is* it?"

He stifled another sigh. "You know my history, how obsessed I was with business that I neglected my wife and my
daughter, and both of them drifted away from me."

Madame Karitska nodded. "Absent father, absent husband.
But your daughter—Laurie—has left that commune in Vermont now, and is back in Trafton at college, isn't she?"

"Yes," he admitted, "and we'd been getting along so well; I visited her there just last week and we had dinner together. Now she's gone."

"Laurie's *gone?*"

He buried his face in his hands. "I should have been more worried when I saw her at college, but she looked . . . looked so *happy,* said she'd finally found what she's always been looking for, a sense of community and *love.* A young man named Derek—not one of the students—had helped her to find it, she said. And I thought—stupidly- -she'd been speaking of being happy at college."

"One would," agreed Madame Karitska. "I take it not?"

He said miserably, "She left two days ago to join a group called the Guardians of Eden, and just sent me a note, didn't even call to tell me. To live there, apparently . . . for a while, she said—this Derek, I suppose. I drove over there at once yesterday afternoon, and I wasn't allowed to see her. 'Come back in a week,' they told me. My *daughter.*"

Madame Karitska had stiffened. "Guardians of Eden," she repeated. "This is not the first time I've heard that name, but who *are* they?"

Faber-Jones lifted his head to say dryly, "Apparently guardians of an Eden devised by another human. Their estate is in Edgerton. I went to the police station there, and asked about them after being turned away."

"And?"

"So far as they know, the place is well financed, by whom they don't know. It's a heavily gated community; the electrician is the only one who's gained entry lately—and left," he added in a worried voice. "I asked the address of the electrician and talked to him last night. He wouldn't say much, didn't want trouble, said they paid him really well but he didn't much like the place. Too many closed doors, he said."

"It's not one of those Armageddon places, is it? The end of the world, and all that?" she asked.

"The police didn't think so, said their motto was 'Peace of the Heart.' " He shook his head. "It's my guess Laurie thought it another hippie commune, like the one she lived in before, in Vermont, which shocked me at the time but seems downright wholesome now in comparison . . . grew their own vegetables, went in for weaving, that sort of thing. If only I could give her what she seems to need!"

Madame Karitska considered this. "If one could remove her, somehow, I can think of how she might find what she needs."

"What? Where?"

But Madame Karitska only shook her head. "She's firmly at Eden for the moment. You mentioned a Derek?"

He nodded. "She met him at college but he's not enrolled there and nobody could tell me his last name. He just hung around the college, they tell me," and added bitterly, "recruiting vulnerable students, no doubt."

Madame Karitska nodded. "Perhaps our friend Pruden might be of some help here."

Faber-Jones brightened. "Of course, of course! He and Jan are coming to my dinner party Sunday; I'll ask him." He rose from the couch to say, "Thank you, thank you for listening. And I'll see you on Sunday."

"Yes," she assured him, smiling. "And with my baklava."

Madame Karitska had been looking forward to Faber-Jones's Sunday dinner party, and being not without her share of vanity she also looked forward to wearing the long brocade skirt she'd found at a flea market. Its shades of pink and mauve became her, and to this she added a black velvet jacket that matched her dark hair, which she wore parted in the center and drawn severely back into a knot.

With the exception of the stranger whom Faber-Jones had mentioned, she was already acquainted with his circle of new friends. There would be his modest and likable medical doctor named Berkowitz, and of course Lieutenant Pruden and his delightful fiancée, Jan Cooper Hyer. His newest addition would be Tanya Jamison, the business manager of his newly formed Pisces Record Company, whom he had enticed away from a very successful recording studio. Already she was promoting Pisces Record Company with instinct and flair, a vivacious young woman whom Madame Karitska had met twice and liked very much.

And to this party she brought herself and her baklava—with hazelnuts, so difficult to find in Trafton.

It was a smaller house on Cavendish Square that Faber-Jones lived in since his wife had left him, but he'd kept his valued cook and her husband with him. The living room was huge, bright with the last of the day's sunshine, and at its farthest end stood a long mahogany refectory table gleaming now with silver candlesticks, place settings, and flowers.

It was Dr. Berkowitz who opened the door to her and greeted her warmly. "Dear Madame Karitska," he said, "how can I ever forget the last dinner party we shared here?"

She smiled. "It was . . . well, surprisingly dramatic, wasn't it. You've been well?"

"As well as one can be at my age," and with an air of mock conspiracy he added, "I hear that our appetitzer is to be quail's-egg tartlets again, which will make us all *very* well indeed."

She laughed. "Mr. Faber-Jones spoils us, doesn't he."

"And you have brought baklava, I hear, but you've missed the latest news . . . Detective Pruden tells us there's been a Brinks robbery today, so we're fortunate he could take the evening off to be with us."

"Fortunate indeed," she said, and having removed her shawl she placed her contribution on a chair until it could be rescued by Faber-Jones's cook.

From the couch Tanya Jamison called, "I hear good news; John Painter's album is just out, and is selling marvelously well."

Jan Cooper Hyer walked over and gave Madame Karitska both a hug and a kiss; Pruden waved and smiled, and Faber-Jones, deep in conversation with the only stranger among them, leaped to his feet, and taking her by the arm led her to him, a tall and trim-looking man with deep-set piercing eyes. Faber-Jones said, "I've already warned everyone how careful we must be; this friend of mine is in intelligence at a *very* high level. Madame Karitska, Roger Gillespie."

"Yes, very dangerous," said Gillespie with a charming smile. "Delighted to meet you."

Over cocktails they made desultory conversation on current politics, and on an outbreak of flu that occupied Dr. Berkowitz, but it was impossible to avoid the news that Pruden had brought to them of a Brinks robbery.

"It's so astonishing that he disappeared," said Tanya. "Tell us the rest of it, Lieutenant Pruden. I mean, you said the man simply vanished, like a Houdini?"

"So far, yes," Pruden said grimly. "And clever, definitely. "They work in twos, you know, making the rounds of banks and stores to collect their money. This man, John Mayfield, made the collections and rode in the back of the Brinks truck between stops. Around half past two their next stop was at a popular restaurant, where his coworker said Mayfield had a crush on one of the waitresses. Mayfield went in, collected the cash and came back, said wait a minute, he had a present to take to the waitress, and he wheeled in a carton labeled 'champagne' and never returned. Seems that during their stops in the morning, while he was in the back, he'd cut open all the bags of cash they'd collected that morning—untraceable cash, no securities—and what he wheeled away was not a case of champagne but a small fortune. If he went into that restaurant nobody saw him, and no one noticed a uniformed Brinks guard anywhere in the neighborhood."

"And he just . . . disappeared?" said Madame Karitska.

Pruden nodded. "After ten minutes his coworker put out an alarm. We have all the airlines watched, and his home under surveillance. Just before I left work his car had been found parked neatly in the Brinks lot."

"What about that waitress?" asked Jan.

He shook his head. "Pure fiction. We were told that he never spoke to any of them, only the manager and the cashier, both men."

Gillespie nodded. "An accomplice, surely, waiting for him in a car?"

Pruden nodded. "Has to be. The search goes on all night, and will be waiting for me tomorrow. We'll find him—have to—if we can't the bonding company will have to make up the loss. But don't let me spoil your appetite," he added with a smile.

It was when they sat down to dinner that Faber-Jones said abruptly, as if he could wait no longer, "I hate to bother you when there's so much on your mind, Lieutenant Pruden, but what do you know about the Guardians of Eden out on Amber Avenue in the Edgerton section?"

"Oh dear," said Jan Cooper Hyer.

"Why 'oh dear'?" demanded Faber-Jones.

Turning to Roger Gillespie, Jan explained, "I work at the Trafton Settlement House," and to Faber-Jones, "We've lost two of our volunteer people to the Guardians of Eden—but I didn't mean to interrupt."

Pruden nodded. "We do know something about it, yes. It's called a retreat, although one of our men rather flippantly refers to it as a Happy Farm, presumably for the disillusioned."

"Who runs it?" asked Madame Karitska.

"A doctor of some sort. Calls himself Brother Robin. He's written a book pretty much condemning the absence of any sense of community in the modern world . . . rather a lot about the need to return to purity of mind and soul, that sort of thing. Why?"

"Because," said Faber-Jones indignantly, "my daughter Laurie seems to have suddenly left college to live there, and when I drove over at once to the estate on Amber Avenue they refused to let me see her. 'Come back in a week,' they said, but I'm not sure I believe them."

Pruden frowned. "That's new to me, and certainly *very* strange, not allowing a father to see his daughter."

Faber-Jones said bitterly, "Afraid they'd lose her, no doubt. She has her own bank account. I'm growing suspicious."

Tanya Jamison nodded. "As any parent would be, yes. It would be interesting to inquire at the bank if she still has her account there, or if it's been emptied."

Pruden said, "If that should be the case, we'll certainly have to look into it." He shook his head. "Gangs we have, unfortunately, but a cult—"

Roger Gillespie said, "Cults can be very attractive these days. We've created such an impersonal and complicated world for our children, too dependent on forces we can't control, leaving us vulnerable, extremely so."

"Vulnerable?" murmured Dr. Berkowitz.

Faber-Jones said, "I might further explain that Roger is our government's top intelligence expert on terrorism."

"Terrorism!" exclaimed Tanya. "We move from robberies to terrorism?"

"Cults often lead to terrorism," pointed out Gillespie, "depending on what their emphasis may be, of course, whether purity of soul or destruction and hate. In Japan, fanatics from the religious cult AUM boarded subway trains with bags of sarin, and in releasing them killed people and injured thousands. And, as you know very well, we've bred our own crop of terrorists: the Oklahoma City bombers, the Heaven's Gate cult, and before that Jim Jones and his mass deaths in Guyana, not to mention Charles Manson earlier, on a smaller scale."

Dr. Berkowitz, frowning, said, "But you mentioned forces we can't control. What did you mean exactly?"

"Tell them, Roger," Faber-Jones said, and to the others, "He's given interviews and talks on this, so it's no secret."

Gillespie nodded. "What I'm saying is that as terrorists grow more sophisticated, and electronic experts more ingenious, as reality becomes 'virtual' reality, we enter a dangerous world."

"Dangerous in what way?" asked Dr. Berkowitz. "Are you thinking of anthrax or sarin or bombs?"

Gillespie shook his head. "Anthrax? To bring an entire country to its knees there would have to be incredible quantities— tons and tons—manufactured, all of it made in laboratories, and you'd no doubt need hundreds of planes to disseminate it. As for bombs, one bomb can kill hundreds in one city and is tragic enough, God knows, but multiply it by city after city—"

Jan said incredulously, "You can't mean these dreadful computer hackers invading us with their viruses, overloading computers, raiding company files . . . I can't believe that!"

Gillespie looked almost amused. "Unfortunately that's what all the CEOs I talk to assume: competent and inventive global hackers making their mischief. No, I'm talking of our dependence on electricity. Can you think of anything in your home that doesn't depend on electricity?"

Tanya said flippantly, "My toothbrush."

He smiled. "Ah, but you rinse with water, don't you, and how do you think water arrives through your pipes?"

"Oh," she said, startled.

"A manual typewriter," ventured Pruden.

"Yes, if you can find one."

"My car?" suggested Dr. Berkowitz.

"A car is refueled at a gas station by pumps that are operated by electricity." Gillespie added dryly, "It's not occurred to us how dependent on one source we've become. My wife, for instance, uses an electric can opener and hair dryer, our gas furnace is triggered by an electric turn-on, my wife and I still enjoy the pleasure of an electric blanket, our sons watch television, when my car needs gas I stop at a gas pump that operates on electricity, as I mentioned . . . I use an electric shaver, and my two daughters spend hours on the Internet, and these rooms we're dining in are blessedly cooled by air-conditioning. We all of us survived the millennium—Y2K—

very nicely, but may not always be so fortunate. After all, what would be left if the genie escapes the bottle?"

Madame Karitska felt a growing unease among the guests and gave him a curious glance.

Dr. Berkowitz said, "Why are you saying this?"

"Yes," said Tanya, "what are you leading up to?"

"To something far worse," he told them, and his face sobered. "What I'm talking about are people capable of shutting down whole cities: 911 calls, lights, transportation systems, elevators. . . . Planes don't fly, trains don't move, *or* the police and the military. Computers and phones go dead. You black out one city, people die. You black out lots of cities, lots of people die. An entire country at a standstill."

"You're scaring me," said Tanya Jamison.

"Good. You should be. We all should be."

"This is a huge country," protested Pruden. "How? How could that be done?"

"I'm not an electronic genius," Gillespie pointed out, "but considering how new electronic devices and inventions multiply month by month . . . Or picture it this way," he said. "An entire generation has grown up reading science-fiction novels and seeing sci-fi movies, where—with the zap of a ray gun—villains and whole cities are wiped out. Consider the equivalent of that ray gun—sonic beams, powerful magnetic charges, who knows? We've been breeding a hotbed of electronic geniuses, really brilliant men and women. It needs only a few 'rogue' geniuses to set up shop very, very privately and come up with a machine more powerful and advanced than

anything known before, one that would connect entirely—
and *only*—to specific targets. Forget computers. Think electric companies . . . power plants and grids, the *source* of all
our power. Kaput. Out of order."

Jan said incredulously, "How horrible. You've said who
might, but *why?*"

"Blackmail. Power. Greed. Ego. The challenge of it. An entire nation rendered helpless."

There was a long and stunned silence until Tanya said
again, "You really *are* frightening us."

He nodded. "It would be an electronic Pearl Harbor, yes." After a moment he added lightly, "On the other hand, in my own
very small department we cultivate and nourish our own forms
of surveillance and watchfulness, which shall be nameless."

Madame Karitska said, "And have you already indications,
suspicions—"

He shrugged. "Mere rumors . . . whispers in the wind, so to
speak. But do let's change the subject now; I've done enough
proselytizing and have become a complete bore."

There followed a long and sober silence until Faber-Jones
broke it by saying, "Actually, Roger's a very normal chap, you
know, devoted to his family and plays a mean game of ten-
nis." With a glance at Madame Karitska he said, "You've not
contributed much to this. Picking up any vibrations?"

"Vibrations?" asked Gillespie.

"She's a very talented psychic—sorry, clairvoyant—as
Lieutenant Pruden can tell you. If you ever need help, there's
your person!"

Obviously he had not confided his own blossoming talent to his friend.

"Really," Gillespie said without interest.

"He flatters me," Madame Karitska told him politely and dismissively.

Pruden glanced at his fiancée and then at Faber-Jones and laughed. "Actually, Mr. Gillespie, you're surrounded by—"

Jan gave him a reproachful glance. "By her admirers," she said firmly.

With equal dismissiveness Gillespie said, "Our department doesn't delve into the supernatural; it's strictly science with us."

But Faber-Jones refused this. "Try her, my friend—I dare you. Just to . . . well, entertain us, if Madame Karitska doesn't feel insulted by the word. After all, you've presented us with a frightening doomsday scenario."

Gillespie laughed. "You fiend . . . All right, if it lightens the moment . . ." He shrugged, and turning to Madame Karitska, "What is it you need for your magic?"

Jan said, "Give her something to hold that's been in your possession for a long time, because what she uses is psychometry."

Gillespie thought a moment and then, loosening his shirt, brought out a small piece of jagged metal laced to a thin leather cord. "All yours," he said with amusement, and handed it to her.

Madame Karitska gave him a quizzical glance and then placed it in her right hand, but loosely because its edges were sharp. She closed her eyes and the room was suddenly very still. Abruptly opening her eyes she said, "This is a very curious piece of metal but it scarcely needs clairvoyance to guess that it's a piece of shrapnel."

His voice was curt. "Scarcely clairvoyance, no."

Again she closed her eyes and for a long moment was silent until she frowned. "All that comes to me— is this really yours? What I'm feeling—the impression I'm receiving from this is so very odd, so removed, so foreign to anyone in your position." She shook her head, still concentrating. "I can feel a searingly hot sun. And thirst. And *fear* . . . walls, crumbling stone walls, yellow, perhaps mud or adobe." She shivered. "I do not like this; there is such *pain*. And fear." With a shudder she opened her eyes. "I'm sorry, I don't understand. Was this a memento from a friend?"

From the look on Gillespie's face she appeared to have shocked him. After a long moment he said soberly, "All right, it's mine, yes. . . . It was a long, long time ago. Africa, a UN mission. Our plane was shot down and we were taken hostage. Five of us survived the crash and we were treated *very* badly. We nearly died." His voice broke. "After we were rescued, that piece of shrapnel was dug out of my thigh. I kept it—prized it—to remind me how precarious life is, and how lucky we were." Turning to Madame Karitska he said, "I hope you will accept my apologies."

She nodded. "Yes, of course," and applied herself to eating her dessert again, aware that he was staring at her, baffled and discomfitted.

He said, "This goes beyond extrasensory perception."

Reluctantly she nodded. "Many people make their decisions with an ESP they don't realize they possess."

"No, this is different. How does it happen? When did it begin?"

"As a child."

"Can you see the future?"

Vehemently she said, "*No*. That is, yes, but I prefer not. I cannot say that mine is a pleasing or comfortable gift to have been given. Only when I see happiness in a future"— she smiled at Pruden—"such as telling *him* he would one day meet and love a young woman with very pale silvery blond hair, who is also—" She did not finish this. "No, very seldom the future. Only the concerns of the present and the past."

The candles on the table had been slowly dimming, and with a sudden glance at his watch Gillespie said, "I had no idea it's grown so late. I'll have to leave, I'm catching the last plane back to Washington."

They all rose from the table, and as they retrieved their coats Tanya said to Gillespie, "You've certainly scared the heck out of us. I think I'll order an extra cord of wood for my fireplace and buy a few kerosene lamps."

Gillespie said dryly, "The best of intentions fade by morning light, when you take a hot shower tomorrow, for instance, snap on a light, draw food from your refrigerator and turn on your computer."

Faber-Jones laughed. "Gillespie does this, you know. Very

insistent man, and not too popular with the State Department. But I'm delighted you could join us, Roger."

"I enjoyed it," he said gravely, but to Madame Karitska, shaking her hand, he said quietly, "If I have frightened Miss Jamison, you—I must admit—have somewhat humbled me."

"Which," said Pruden with a smile, "makes it a perfect dinner party, a stimulating if *quite* alarming evening."

10

It was the next afternoon that Faber-Jones telephoned Madame Karitska to say in an anguished voice, "I wasn't fast enough, Tanya was right, Laurie's bank account was closed out yesterday, very late in the afternoon."

"By Laurie personally?" she asked.

"Yes, but a young man was with her," he said. "I questioned the woman, the officer who handles the closing of accounts. It's a small bank, a branch of the main one, and near the college, so Laurie had often cashed checks there, and the woman recognized her. She's so pretty, you know . . . Laurie, I mean. I asked for details and when she thought about it she said Laurie seemed to her overexcited, her eyes very bright."

"And the young man with her?"

"I've got his description," he said grimly. "I have to wait now to see who she endorsed the check to. As if I can't guess," he added angrily.

"You've spoken with Pruden?"

"Caught him on the wing, so to speak. Of course he's knee-deep in the Brinks robbery but he did ask the name of the electrician I talked with."

"Which means that eventually—"

Faber-Jones sighed. "Eventually, yes. If he remembers."

But he had misjudged Pruden. After a day of failure to discover any traces of John Mayfield, the FBI arrived to take over the investigation. The Trafton police turned over their limited results to them, and three days later Pruden put in a call to Joe Witkowski at the Amber Avenue Electric Company to ask when he might see him.

"At day's end, five o'clock," the man said, and Pruden found him at five o'clock in his shop, washing his hands with yellow soap, still in a bright blue overall with JOE'S ELECTRIC printed in blazing white across the back.

"Police, hmm?" he said, looking at him narrowly.

Pruden, not in uniform, nodded and showed him his badge. "We're interested in the Guardians of Eden. We hear you've done some electrical work for them, according to a Mr. Faber-Jones, whose daughter has suddenly joined them. It upset him very much."

"Aye," said Joe, nodding. "Him I recall, he came to see me. Upset, like any dad would be."

"Can you describe the place?"

"I don't want trouble," Joe said. "I just found it spooky but they pay damn well. Maybe I went at the wrong times of the day—I've wired three rooms for them at the top of the place—but considering how many people there must be in that big house it was always damned silent. That's what bugged me. No sound of voices. Doors closed." He shrugged. "Maybe it was naptime, who knows? The man who took me upstairs the first time wore a robe, of all things. And long hair." He shook his head. "I've got a son with long hair but he's sixteen.... There's something about grown-up men with long hair that strikes me as damn silly."

"You've got to admit it's good theater," said Pruden.

Witkowski laughed. "Aye, that's the point of it, isn't it." He looked Pruden over carefully. "I'm booked to go back on Tuesday. If you know anything about tools you could come along and work with me. Look the place over."

"I can change a lightbulb," Pruden told him dryly, "and I did take shop in high school and know a wrench from a screwdriver."

Witkowski went to his cluttered desk and drew from the pile of catalogs, calendars, bills, and receipts a colorful advertisement, illustrated, of small tools. Handing it to him he said, "Look these over; it has pictures of screws, pointers, brads, and so on. Come for coffee at seven-fifteen Tuesday morning; I'll have an overall and cap for you and we'll leave seven-thirty on the dot."

"Great," said Pruden. "And thanks."

Early on Tuesday, having done his homework, Pruden met Joe at his shop, had a very good cup of coffee, and they set out in his van for the Amber Avenue estate. "Used to be the old Governor Stuyvesant mansion," confided Joe. "Just wait until you see it now."

It was just as well that Pruden had been forewarned: the house had been remodeled—by a madman, surely—into an architectural monstrosity, a mixture of New England and the Mediterranean: there were arched Moorish windows, several charming ironwork balconies, but a very New England

widow's walk on the roof, all this set on a grassy knoll surrounded by a high wrought-iron fence with a gate on which
an intercom was mounted.

Joe reached out and pressed the button on the intercom
and a pleasant voice said, "Guardians of Eden . . . State your
name, please."

Once he'd been identified, the gate slowly opened and
they drove up to the front door, where they were met by a
young man wearing what looked like a burlap robe (*sackcloth
and ashes?* wondered Pruden). The young man nodded to
Joe, glanced doubtfully at Pruden, and then led them
through wide halls and up three flights of stairs to a room at
the top of the house, a white room bare of furnishings.

"There you are," he said "Lavatory two doors down," and
he left.

In a low voice Pruden said, "How many rooms *are* there in
this house?"

"Twenty-five at least; I looked it up in the library's Historical Room. And they must be filling up fast to be developing
this top floor, which is why they've brought me in." Unpacking his tools Joe brought out a diagram he'd apparently been
given on earlier trips, and became very busy drilling holes for
outlets, running snakelike connections behind the wall and
repeating this process in silence while Pruden handed him
tools and kept very quiet.

Finally, "Lavatory," he told Joe, feeling it time to recon-
noiter, and strolled down the hall toward the bathroom. Passing several closed doors he quietly opened one of them an
inch or two. What he saw were six or seven young women in

white robes lying on mats on the floor, eyes closed, an older woman crouched over them and intoning in a soft, dulcet, singsong voice ". . . to feel at one with the universe, and bathed in love . . . can you feel the warmth of our love . . . *Love* . . . at last you have reached *home.*"

"*Home,*" the girls repeated drowsily.

Pruden quietly closed the door and stood in the hall, frowning. He looked at the three other closed doors and he wondered . . . but someone was coming up the staircase and he tiptoed back to Joe.

Joe gave him a quick glance and handed him a pair of pliers. "Hold the end of this wire," he said in a low voice. "Look busy." In a louder voice, "I need a 1¼ brad. And I can use those 7/16 pointers to hold the wire."

Joe's ears had been even more attuned than his to the sound of footsteps. "Nearly finished?" asked a man in the doorway.

Over his shoulder Pruden glanced at him and quickly, professionally, memorized him: tall, over six feet, rose-colored robe and sandals, sensual mouth, beak of a nose; heavy brows; dark hair flecked with gray; he decided this must be Brother Robin.

"Almost," called out Joe to the man, and pinning a last wire to the molding said, "There!" Rising, he rubbed his hands together, glanced over the job, and nodded. "All done," he said.

"You didn't bring a helper last time," the man told him curtly.

Joe said amiably, "Save you money, my bringing Pete— finished in half the time."

"You can send us the bill as usual," the man told him, and waited while Joe packed up his tools and handed his toolbox to Pruden. "All set," he said cheerfully.

The man, waiting, led them personally down the staircase past a room where a dozen people stood with raised arms, swaying back and forth and softly chanting what Pruden gathered was a mantra, but their host quickly closed the door before Pruden could see faces.

The massive front door was opened for them and they walked out to Joe's truck; he placed the tools in back and they climbed in. As the car started Pruden saw the man in the rose-colored robe still watching them.

"Gives me the creeps," Joe said once the gate opened for them and they turned onto the street.

"Me, too," admitted Pruden. "At least I've gotten the feel of the place, and I thank you for it. So just what were we wiring?"

"You know, that's a very interesting question," said Joe. "I've wired three rooms by now, all the same, a crazy setup, most of the wires running out of sight behind the walls and up to the ceiling and an incredible number of outlets. . . . The only possibility I can think of for such a setup, the only one possible . . ."

"Yes?" asked Pruden, as he hesitated.

"Listening devices. I suspect he plans to bug every room."

"Good God," said Pruden. "Not good, not good at all."

"Not if anyone gets restless and wants to leave." With a quick glance at him Joe said, "Police interested?"

"Only me. So far."

Joe nodded, and added casually, "I'm booked to wire the last room on Friday, a two-hour job this time, smaller room. Care to come?"

"Definitely," said Pruden.

The chief had originally refused to authorize Pruden's research into the Guardians of Eden but had finally relented. Now he demanded, "So just what do you think's going on out there?" His voice was skeptical.

"Whatever it is, I don't like it," Pruden told him. "Possibly drugs. The one group I very briefly spotted sounded half-asleep and kept drowsily repeating, 'home . . . home . . .'" like the sound track in the film *E.T.*"

"No fingers pointed skyward?" said the chief sardonically. "Aliens from another planet? Scarcely worth our attention."

Pruden sighed. "Nevertheless, two of Jan's volunteers at the Settlement House are there, as well as Faber-Jones's daughter, who took with her twenty-one thousand dollars from her savings account."

"Yes, but can you *prove* the girl's there?" demanded the chief. "Did you see her there? Did her father? How do you know she's not run off with a boyfriend on a well-financed joyride, and used the name of that place to cover her tracks?"

"I can't," admitted Pruden. "But I can tell you that it looks to me as if anyone who *is* there is not likely to leave, even if they want to."

"Prove it," said the chief. "You tell me Joe Witkowski thinks what he's installing will be used for eavesdropping, but he can't prove that, either, can he?"

With a sigh Pruden admitted defeat and rose to go. Before he reached the door the chief said less harshly, "Look here, I trust your instincts, Pruden. If you learn anything tangible I'll listen, but we need *proof*. Oh, and by the way—"

Pruden stopped and turned.

"About the diamonds stored in our safe? We heard this morning from the police in New York. The dealers in the Manhattan Diamond District have been very helpful; they tracked down the company in Antwerp this Verlag chap worked for, but it seems he left them a year and a half ago. The Antwerp police are asking us to send the attaché case to them by courier. They're very suspicious about this Georges Verlag—have been for some time. It seems that diamonds have characteristics that can prove whether or not these are De Beers gems or whether Verlag was into smuggling diamonds out of Sierra Leone by way of Liberia, in which case he's been illegally abetting some very cutthroat rebels and is not the man your what's-her-name friend thought he was."

Pruden grinned. Even now the chief had difficulty acknowledging Madame Karitska. "Bad news," he agreed.

"Yes. You'll have to tell her."

Pruden nodded and left. He would later stop in to see the chief's "what's-her-name," but as to Faber-Jones he felt that to admit and describe his visit to the Guardians of Eden would only alarm him more than it did Pruden.

Leaving his desk at half past five Pruden realized that before meeting Jan for dinner there was still time to stop and give Madame Karitska news of Georges Verlag. He found her door ajar, with a sign, BACK IN 5 MINUTES, and he guessed that she must be upstairs seeing her landlord. Since her door was open he walked in and headed for a couch, realizing how tired he was, and he stretched out, relaxing, a sense of her presence still lingering. Except for books added to the shelves that lined one wall the room had not changed in the year that he'd known her, and he thought how much he appreciated the calm he felt here. He need only walk up the steps of the shabby brownstone, past the sign in the window, enter, and knock on her door to enter this other world. The wall of books muted the sound of traffic outside, the high-ceilinged room was cool, and there were always flowers on the carved coffee table; a room that should have been gloomy, considering its location and size, was as bright and cheerful as Madame Karitska.

Hearing her steps on the staircase he rose, and at sight of him she smiled. "Paying my rent," she told him. "What can I do for you?"

He said, "I came to tell you that your friend Georges Verlag is not quite the respectable man you remember from your European past."

She smiled. "I expected to hear this from you. You've heard from Europe?"

"Expected? You *knew*?"

She said quietly, seating herself on the couch opposite his, "I've been remembering him as he was in Antwerp: a large young man, a little stooped, and very shy. He liked my cooking but hardly spoke to me. I fear that I found him boring and looked no closer. . . . I was a nonpracticing psychic in those days, and there had been difficulties in my marriage."

Pruden, thoroughly puzzled, said, "I'm not following this."

She hesitated and then said, "I think you could be trusted, as a friend, not a policeman . . . I'd like you to see the letter I received from Georges Verlag yesterday, but only if you pledge silence."

Aghast, he said, "Letter? from *Verlag*? and silence when all the police in Europe are looking for him?"

"Too *many* people looking for him," and her gaze at him was so serious and stern that Pruden found himself saying, "All right, I can forget I'm a policeman *unless*—"

"Read it," she said, and handed the envelope to him.

With a glance at the postmark he said, "*République Algérienne*, I see . . . he's in Algeria, then?" Opening it he read, " 'My dear Marina, I was very touched that you remembered and recognized me in Trafton. You rescued me at a very, very dangerous moment and I owe you a life that I expect to be losing soon; in fact when you receive this I may already be dead. I want you to know that you did not rescue a dishonorable man on the subway that day; my work has been so highly confidential that only a very few in Europe know that I have been working undercover. To identify and report on the horrors perpetuated by greedy men in Kasengo. It would comfort me at the death I sense is waiting for me to know that you of all people not think ill of me. . . . Humbly, Georges V.' "

Pruden placed the letter back on the table. " 'Humbly,' " he repeated. "So all the accusations made of him have been deliberate, to protect him?"

She nodded. "It would seem so, yes. His letter has made me very sad for him, it touched me deeply."

Pruden frowned. "It affected me as well, and if this is true," he said, "and I feel it true, there will be two people who don't think ill of him."

"But only two," she reminded him sternly.

"Only we two," he agreed. "Do you think he's still alive?"

"I don't think I'll ever know, do you? I certainly didn't 'read' him very well in Antwerp, did I . . . too many difficulties, and my husband making reckless investments . . ." Her voice faded; she shook herself of regrets and firmly returned her attention to Pruden. "But my impressions are not blocked today, or in Trafton, and I think, my friend, that you have had a very angry day."

He sighed. "It shows?" He told her of his contacting Joe Witkowski and of their visit to the Guardians of Eden that morning. "I'm angry, yes," he admitted. "I'm angry because I'm very suspicious, and helpless because there's nothing that can be done without proof." He shook his head. "I'm really quite fond of Faber-Jones and he's going to make himself sick with worry, and the chief rightly points out that nothing can be done without proof. Search warrants need proof."

Madame Karitska looked thoughtful. "What sort of proof might be needed?"

"I wish I knew. Give me a search warrant—somehow—and I'd look for drugs, I'm sure they're there. Look for names, documents, records . . ."

"But they wouldn't dare keep records, would they?" she asked.

"Not if they're smart. Aside from sneaking in an undercover agent . . ." He shook his head. "They're too smart for that, too, I'm sure. Anyway, Joe's due to go back on Friday to wire the last room and I'm determined to go with him, with or without the chief's permission." He glanced at his watch and gave a start. "Got to go, I'm meeting Jan for dinner." He leaped from the couch and hurried to the door, where he suddenly stopped and turned to look at her. "We've still got a 'Wanted' out on the man following Verlag that day when he tossed his attaché case to you. *That* remains Trafton's business, and a police matter, but we'll keep Verlag's name out of it."

"Very sensible"—Madame Karitska nodded—"since I'm reasonably certain that he'd have killed Georges for those diamonds." She added thoughtfully, "You might try Amos Herzog. When I described the man to Amos he thought it sounded like a man called Frankie the Ferret."

Pruden looked shocked. "You know Amos Herzog?"

She laughed at the expression on his face. "Yes, we're old friends."

"*Amos Herzog?*"

"Good-bye, Pruden," she told him firmly. "Say hello to Jan, and give her my love."

11

Pruden managed the next day to corner the chief alone, which was no easy task since most of the building seemed to have been taken over by the FBI men who had poured into Trafton this week. Actually he found the chief in the men's room, where he asked if he might take Friday morning off from duty.

"A hell of a place to ask," the chief told him indignantly.

"How else?" pointed out Pruden.

The chief sighed. "Okay, what is it that needs a morning off?"

"No comment."

He was looked at with suspicion. "Meaning that it's not a family emergency, nobody's died, but whatever you plan my answer would be no?"

Pruden grinned. "Exactly."

The chief sighed. "Well, I'm going slightly crazy with this Brinks investigation, we all are, but you've done your share, so take the damn morning off. Give you a rest from checking every pickpocket and ex-criminal in the city, but be back by noon."

"Yes, sir," and Pruden left before he could change his mind.

And so, once again, but on Friday this time, Pruden made the trip to Joe's Electric, pondering this obsession that had overtaken him in regard to the Guardians of Eden. He simply couldn't rid himself of an uneasy feeling that he could only call instinct, and this was something that had served him well in the past. It was true that he'd found the place claustrophobic, if not downright spooky, but there was nothing he could pin down except for the fact that no one appeared to leave the Guardians of Eden . . . enter but not leave. He thought there had to be a *few* members among the many converts who became disillusioned or rebellious and who wanted to get out; the question was, did they discover they couldn't?

It was this that bothered him, because if this was true there had to be drugs to pacify the recalcitrant and tame any troublemakers. In his estimation the place ought to be raided if he could find proof of this.

Joe greeted him cheerfully, handed him a mug of coffee and said, "I'm impressed. You're a stubborn man."

Pruden nodded. "And probably a damn fool, but let's go."

On this day as they entered the house, led by the same young man in a brown robe, Pruden thought he must be wrong, after all, because through the window beyond the staircase he could see a dozen men of varying ages doing calisthenics on the rear lawn, a voice shouting, "one two three, one two three . . ."

"Not so quiet," murmured Joe, grinning.

"No," said Pruden.

The room on the top floor was next to the one that Joe had wired two days ago; it smelled of fresh paint, a desk had been brought in, and a stepladder leaned against one wall. Their escort nodded without speaking, and Joe began unpacking his tools while Pruden set up the ladder. Climbing the ladder Joe told him briskly, "Hand me the drill, will you?"

Pruden, somewhat more knowledgeable now, was able to identify and hand up tools to Joe, and take them down, and after forty-five minutes of this—his eyes on his watch—decided it was time to do some reconnoitering. "Off to the lavatory," he told Joe, and Joe nodded, understanding.

Once in the hallway, Pruden passed three closed doors on his left and entered the lavatory on the right, where he flushed the toilet in case the walls had ears, and wondered which of the three doors opposite him in the hall he would dare to open.

Making his exit he confronted those doors, moved toward them, hesitated, and then as he stood there in his bright blue overalls emblazoned with JOE'S ELECTRIC, one of the three doors opened and a man in a brown robe and sandals walked out, gave Pruden's uniform a vague glance and headed for the staircase, but not before Pruden had clearly seen his face. Pruden watched him go in a state of shock, feeling literally stunned. He had hoped to glimpse Faber-Jones's daughter, he had hoped to find some hint of drugs, but he'd not expected *this*. He had to be wrong, had to be, but he knew he wasn't; he had just seen a man the police and the FBI had been hunting for nearly a week, and whose face was already appearing all over the country with the word *Wanted* on it.

It was the Brinks robber, John Mayfield.

And *here*, of all places? *This* was how he had so miraculously vanished?

Pruden stood rooted, his thoughts spinning in circles as he tried to puzzle this out. . . . Did Brother Robin know he was harboring a criminal? Surely he couldn't know that, yet there had to have been a car—something or *someone*—waiting near the Coronado Café to whisk Mayfield away, and that meant an accomplice . . . could that accomplice have been Brother Robin? Who *was* Brother Robin? Surely Mayfield couldn't be here at the Guardians of Eden without his cooperation. Had the two of them plotted the Brinks robbery together, or had Mayfield simply come to him as a disciple, offering a fortune?

Pruden found himself cynically recalling the list of Mayfield's friends whom they'd been interviewing, all their queries horribly wrong, always about a waitress or Mayfield's past, when they should have asked if Mayfield had ever mentioned the Guardians of Eden.

But who would have thought of *this*?

Hastily he returned to Joe, who gave him an odd glance and said, "You look like you've seen a ghost."

"I have," Pruden said grimly. "Nearly finished? We've got to get the hell out of here."

"Okay with me," Joe said, and packed up his tools and they quietly left.

Once in his own car Pruden turned on the siren and drove beyond the speed limit in his haste to reach headquarters. Leaving his car parked next to a No Parking sign he dashed into the building, and too impatient to wait for an elevator, took the stairs two at a time to the chief's office, where he told the fierce-looking secretary who guarded him, "Got to see him."

She looked at him pityingly. "You know you can't, he's in conference with a man from the FBI, and why didn't you take the elevator; you look terrible, Lieutenant."

"Sorry," he said, and deaf to her protests, he strode past her and into the chief's office, startling the two occupants of the room.

His chief said sharply, "I gave strict orders—"

"I've found him," blurted out Pruden.

The chief glanced at his companion apologetically, and to Pruden, with a sigh, said patiently, "Found who?"

"John Mayfield."

If he had produced one reproachful glance and one furious glance, he was now rewarded by seeing one man jump to his feet and his chief's mouth drop open.

"What do you mean, you've found him?" demanded the chief.

"He's at the Guardians of Eden wearing a long brown robe and sandals."

The FBI man said, "Guardians of *what*?" and turning to the chief, "What the hell is he talking about?"

"Are you sure?" asked the chief. "So that's where you went this morning! Did he see you?"

"He saw only my blue overalls, Joe's Electric," he told him. "Uniforms are remarkably anonymous."

"You'd better sit down," suggested the chief, and with a nod to his companion, "This is Frank Johnson . . . Johnson, Lieutenant Pruden."

The chief ordered coffee, and a serious discussion began.

Johnson said, "I'll want to see the house—a drive-by sighting—but give me a rough sketch of it now."

"Right," said Pruden, and with a sheet of paper and a pencil began to block out the shape and size of it. "According to my friend Joe, the electrician," he explained, "it was once the Governor Stuyvesant mansion before someone eccentric bought it and jazzed it up. Joe was intrigued enough to look up its history in the library's Historical Room. There's a book there with pictures of it, inside and out."

The chief nodded. "We can use that."

Pruden had sketched while he talked and now handed it over, saying, "Here you are."

"Hmmm," murmured Johnson. "We could storm that place easily enough."

Pruden said, "I wouldn't advise that."

He received a cold glance. "May I ask why not?"

"That six-foot-high fence has an electric gate with an intercom. They'd be warned. I've seen Brother Robin and it's my belief . . ." He hesitated. "It's my belief that he's not one to give up easily, he's more likely to set the place on fire or blow it up, and the house is full of perfectly innocent converts who don't deserve to die—in fact by this time half of them may wish they'd never fallen for his propaganda of

peace, community, love, and whatever he promised them."
He added politely, "And of course you'd never retrieve the
Brinks money."

The chief said, "That's quite a speech from Pruden, Johnson, I suggest you hear him."

Johnson nodded. "I'm listening, and he has a point there."
To Pruden he added, "But it's John Mayfield we want, that's
why we're here."

Always the money, Pruden sighed, and said dryly, "Your
man can't afford to leave, you know that. I'd say he's there for
a long, long time."

"He could change his appearance and disappear in a
week."

"Do you really think Brother Robin would *let* him go?"
asked Pruden. "There's a lot at stake here, and a lot of money
involved, and Mayfield's hiding there with nearly a million in
untraceable cash. . . . Given time, it's my guess Brother
Robin will slip Mayfield an overdose of drugs and do away
with him . . . kill him . . . unless Mayfield gets desperate and
beats him to it. We're assuming the two are partners in a
crime, and partners in crime usually move from triumph to
greed; we've seen it happen."

"True enough," agreed Johnson. "One wonders if Mayfield knew what he was getting into, not to mention how they
met . . . Brinks very thoroughly investigates their men."

The chief wasn't interested in this. He said thoughtfully,
"Aside from the gate, the house itself could have an interior
alarm system; I'll have several of my men check every company in Trafton that installs interior alarms." Pressing a but-

ton on his intercom he said, "Suzy, get me Swope and Margolies, and after that order me a plain car from the garage."
To Pruden and Johnson he said, "Margolies for the library, to
photocopy all he can find on the layout of the mansion, and
Swope to collect men to interview every company in the book
that installs alarms . . ." He smiled one of his rare smiles.
"Shall I order sandwiches and more coffee, gentlemen, while
we wait?"

When they met again it was Saturday morning and
they had accumulated more information. The hunt
for Mayfield remained in place; Pruden agreed with the chief
it was a waste of men, but word might somehow reach the
Guardians of Eden if it became known the search had been
called off. Swope and his men had found no sign of any cen-
tral alarm systems having been installed. "They must depend
on the fences," he told the chief. The book from the library
was far more helpful than expected; besides photos there was
an actual diagram of the first floor, the rooms labeled maid's
room, changing room, library, front parlor, back parlor,
kitchen and pantry, mudroom, butler's pantry.

Johnson, his mind relentlessly on the Brinks money, studied the diagram with interest. "I'd guess this smaller room at
the back is where you'd find the safe. It's human nature, safes
being as heavy as they are, to establish them on the first floor
rather than to use pulleys and five or six men to haul them
upstairs. At least we can hope that's where it is."

This did not noticeably cheer up the chief, who said sardonically, "So all we need is a safecracker."

Johnson nodded. "And a real pro. I know of a first-rate man for the job but unfortunately he's on assignment in San Francisco. I can think of one or two others but it needs a real gift, this job, and we can't take any chances. Have anyone in your police force?"

The chief sighed. "Only gifted amateurs, but for a job like this . . . Of course we have in Trafton the famous—or infamous—Amos Herzog. He did some lecturing for you some years back, didn't he?"

Johnson said dryly, "A relic from the days when jewel thieves were actually considered heroes if they outwitted the police and didn't carry guns. Yes, I believe he gave a lecture or two some time ago, and then I gather he felt he'd done enough to amuse us and retired. *Really* retired."

Pruden heard this with fresh interest, still reeling from Madame Karitska's calm announcement that he was a friend of hers. He said politely, "I've read some of his books."

"He'd be the one if we could get him," said the chief. "Would a little blackmail bring him out of retirement? or a few subtle threats?"

"Maybe, just maybe," said Pruden, "how about a *friend* of his?"

"Such as?" countered the chief.

Pruden instead asked, "Would he still be good? Would he have lost his touch?"

"What friend?" demanded the chief.

Johnson said crossly, "Never mind who he is; I say try him. If he can persuade Herzog . . . you know this friend?" When Pruden nodded he said, "Good. There's one more contribution I can make. You worry about this Brother Robin blowing up the place? My men can put together a pocket-size fire alarm to be set off as soon as the job's done. *That* should get everyone out in a hurry. If Herzog can be persuaded."

"*If*," said the chief pointedly.

"So that," said Madame Karitska, "is the story I bring you of a blossoming cult in Trafton in which the Brinks robber is hiding."

Amos Herzog looked at her with a twinkle in his eye. "I wondered why you called to ask if I'd invite you for tea this afternoon."

"Well, you did hobnob with the FBI at one time, didn't you? Teach a class or lecture on picking locks?"

"Only because it amused me," he told her. "But I'm certainly curious as to why they sent *you*. Of course, you're far more attractive than the chief of police, but still—"

"Because," she admitted, "I made the mistake of mentioning to Lieutenant Pruden that I know you."

He nodded. "Ah yes, that mysterious policeman who consults you."

"Yes, and they really need an experienced and professional safecracker, and the FBI apparently felt you were unapproachable and very retired."

"So," he said, "you are proposing that I leave my bed in the middle of the night to dismantle an elaborately designed electric gate and intercom, then make my way to the rear of this mansion, climb through a window and break open a safe."

She said with dignity, "I'm sure you're far too skillful to 'break' open a safe; surely you're more subtle."

"My dear Marina—"

"I thought it might amuse you," she said with a shrug.

He threw up his hands. "Deliver me from devious and cunning women! And if I should agree to this mad undertaking just what would I get in return?"

"Absolution?" she suggested with a smile.

"Not enough." He shook his head.

"Then what?" she asked.

"I've heard your proposal; now you can hear mine. There is something you could do for me in return if I agree to this lamentable caper."

"Such as?"

"Consider a proposal of *mine*."

"Such as what?"

His eyes were twinkling again. "A proposal of marriage."

"You? Me?" Utterly astonished she said, "My dear Amos, you're not treating this police matter at all seriously; you have to be joking."

"On the contrary," he told her, "I have been appalled to see you living in such . . . such *penury*. It offends me. You're a very handsome woman, and what's more a very interesting woman, and you don't belong on Eighth Street . . . but I see that I've startled you?"

"You certainly have," she told him. "You wretch, you know very well that I'm perfectly happy living on Eighth Street."

He nodded. "That's what particularly pleases me, since

I've no interest in rescuing anyone out of charity. I'll agree to this if you in turn agree to consider *my* proposal. Note the word *consider*."

"You're quite mad," she told him amiably, "and I don't for a moment believe that you're serious. I'm quite fond of you, I enjoy your company and our occasional chats on the phone evenings, but I've thought of you only as an interesting friend."

"And what better basis for a marriage?" he inquired.

"Amos," she told him, "you've never in your entire life been married."

"Call me a late bloomer."

She smiled. "I'd call you a blackmailer."

"Not at all," he assured her blandly. "I simply asked you to consider my suggestion, to let it simmer for a while in that busy head of yours. As for *your* proposal, I admit that I'd find it gloriously ironic to work for the police. A new experience . . . I'll do it. Is that settled?"

"Yes," she said, and wondered why she suddenly blushed. "They'll be happy to hear this, and you'll probably be having more visitors inside of an hour."

"I hope not in uniform," he said tartly. "After all, I have my reputation to consider."

There were always pedestrians on Amber Avenue, and on the following afternoon a man wearing a baseball cap and shabby trousers gave the fence and the gate a lingering and interested glance. Later a man in a business suit and hat strolled past and stopped to look admiringly at the Governor Stuyvesant house; after a moment he drew out a camera and took several pictures of it.

An hour later a man with a cane, all in black, passed the mansion, stumbled, clung to the gate for a minute and then, drawing himself up slowly, limped away until a block later he entered Pruden's parked car.

"Need any more trips?" asked Pruden.

Herzog shook his head. "They definitely operate the gates from inside the house. What I need now are the photos I took of the wires connecting both intercom and gate. Have the photos been blown up—enlarged—yet?"

"Working on them now; we'll go and see," Pruden told him, and glanced at the man beside him, still intrigued by his sheer audacity. It was an interesting face: white hair and black brows, and those vivid blue eyes. A suave and sophisticated man. He supposed this was how he'd been able to scout prospects in the most expensive shops in Paris, London, New York . . . a glance at a credit card, a moment next to a woman in furs giving her address to a clerk. . . . That at least was what he'd heard of his technique, and always daylight robberies and without a weapon. A risk taker. And damn skillful, too; at headquarters the FBI had already tried him on the most complicated of locks; it had been incredible the speed with which he'd dissembled them. He was a man who applied his obviously keen intelligence to crime, and Pruden wondered what he'd have become if he'd been anything but a jewel thief.

A lot was riding on this man next to him, he reflected, but

he was still wondering how on earth he and Madame Karitska had ever met.

By midnight they were all in position. They'd taken over the house across the street from the mansion, putting the family up in a hotel for the night and using the two front rooms as a stakeout. It was a time of shadows on a dark night . . . a shadowy figure clipping wires at the gate, the gate quietly opening, and Herzog, followed by Pruden, slipping through it, closing it, and in crouch position the two making their way around the house to the rear . . . a shadow at the window as it was pried open—Herzog slipping through . . . the thin beam of a flashlight shining on a safe—Johnson had guessed right about its location—and the astonishing moment when a carton labeled CHAMPAGNE, still heavy with money, was slipped though the window to Pruden, followed by the safe's being emptied of bags of money and documents.

And then Herzog vanished, leaving Pruden to guard the contents of the safe outside, with only the sound of crickets and from the woods the shrill of locusts. Pruden waited nervously for the fire alarm, hoping it worked, and then came the triumph of a shout from Herzog, "Fire! Out! Out!" and the shriek of the alarm . . . and as policemen poured through the unlocked gate to surround the mansion they were accompanied by the sound of screams, doors opening . . . shadowy figures rushing out of the mansion's doors . . . a sudden movement at the top of the house, where someone had rushed to the widow's walk high above him, and as Pruden watched in horror a man threw himself from the top of the house to the ground . . . lights suddenly were on everywhere, showing the mansion's inhabitants in clusters on the lawn, shivering in the night air, all of them relieved to be ushered to safety from what they thought was a mansion on fire.

There were two surprising discoveries from their raid: the appearance of Herzog escorting Brother Robin down the stairs and saying, "Darned if Brother Robin isn't Charley Schumacher, we shared a cell in jail once."

The other discovery, much sadder, was the one casualty of the night, the man who had leaped suicidally from the roof, and they would never know why. His name was Alpha Oliver.

12

Pruden knew that, as usual, Madame Karitska would probably have heard nothing of the raid on the Guardians of Eden, since she rejected television and newspapers. As he understood it, this was akin to "keeping her arteries clear," and Jan, who had been born with the sixth sense, too, laughed at him for describing it so meanly. "You know very well how she explained it," she told him. "She has a gift that she uses five or six days a week now, and even *you* complain about all the crime news and violent programs. She can't afford the *clutter.*"

To which Pruden had said, somewhat worried, "Is this going to happen to you, too?"

With a laugh she had assured him that she intended to live a very normal life. "As I'm sure Marina did until—how can I describe it?—until she was given a sign that she was to use her clairvoyance; go public, so to speak."

"And what was the sign?" Pruden asked, curious.

"Well—or so she told me once, after you all rescued me— she dreamed for two or three nights of a brownstone house with a bright yellow door, and several days later when she went for a walk during one of her free hours she found herself on Eighth Street passing a brownstone with a bright yellow door. In fact, Kristan had just finished painting the door and was very startled to find a tenant so fast." She laughed. "When she told him that she gave readings he actually thought she was a Christian Scientist."

Now they had been invited to dinner that evening, Madame Karitska had promised them a quiche if they would tell her everything that had happened the night before. When they arrived she had set up a table by the window, on which there was room for a small bouquet of flowers and for Pruden and Jan Cooper Hyer to dine comfortably with her.

"I've already had a phone call from Faber-Jones," she told them, "but only to tell me he has Laurie with him, and she's all right, but nothing more. How did your raid go; what happened and what did you find? I'm eager to hear."

"I'm still in a rage," Pruden said.

Jan nodded. "I guess we all thought Brother Robin might be someone such as Roger Gillespie talked about, a cult ready to blow up the world."

Pruden said grimly, "Well, he's blown up the world for a lot of people. He was nothing but a fraud, a damn clever con man. Nothing saintly about him at all. We know now that he came to Trafton six years ago with money from who knows what or whom, rented the Stuyvesant mansion, had a book printed, gave a few lectures—"

"And a radio interview," put in Jan. "At least one that I happened to hear on our local station, and he was certainly persuasive."

Pruden nodded. "Persuasive enough so that having achieved sixty-three followers who lived there, fifty-two of them had turned over their life savings to him—and some were wealthy—all of them prepared to live and die there with him, or so they believed."

"Persuasive indeed," murmured Madame Karitska.

"Unfortunately there was not the slightest hint or breath of the spiritual about Guardians of Eden," said Pruden. "Somewhere he'd acquired the vocabulary of a guru and he was selling love, belonging and community like a salesman, but what he was after—like any thief—was money. And," he added, "from what we've found in his safe we figure he'd netted roughly twelve million."

"Twelve million!" Jan gasped. "You didn't tell me that."

"We've only known it for a few hours."

"And were there drugs, as you suspected?" asked Madame Karitska.

"Oh yes, I was right about that; we found quantities of the drug Ecstasy, *very* illegal. It's how he kept the rebellious ones under control. But here's the cruelest part: he made sure that no one could leave the Guardians of Eden, but under intense questioning at headquarters overnight he's admitted that *he* planned to leave in another year. Just walk out—leave, abandoning all of his sixty-three followers with nothing but disillusionment, heartbreak and no money . . . sixty-three personal tragedies."

"And the realization," said Madame Karitska softly, "of how gullible they'd been."

"Which is probably the saddest of all," agreed Pruden. "We've charged him with larceny, fraud, and illegal possession of drugs."

"Good," said Jan.

"And the Brinks robber?" asked Madame Karitska.

Pruden frowned. "Jail for him, too, of course, but he's the strangest of all, because he had a very clean record—had to, or Brinks would never have hired him. Not even a speeding ticket, *nothing*. We've no idea yet how or where he met Brother Robin; he's not talking—in fact they've had to put a suicide watch on him." He gave Madame Karitska a curious glance. "Your friend Amos Herzog was pretty incredible, but I must say he's shockingly frank about his prison background." He suddenly grinned. "I've saved the fun part for the last. Herzog took one look at Brother Robin and said he was Charley Schumacher; he'd shared a cell in jail with him once, long ago, except in those days he was 'Duct Tape Charley.' "

Madame Karitska smiled. "Yes, he's said he found it very educational, his two experiences in prison." She did not add that he remained in touch with some of his old prison friends lest Pruden look on him as a mine of information, which would be *quite* unfair.

"But . . . *Duct Tape* Charley?" exclaimed Jan.

Pruden smiled. "Apparently he was called that years ago, before he learned the more subtle forms of crime; he'd enter a house and silence its occupants by taping their mouths, ankles and wrists with duct tape while he proceeded in leisurely fashion to collect their money and jewelry."

"Rather crude," said Jan, "considering what he must have

learned since then, to present himself as Brother Robin of the Guardians of Eden. But what will happen to his victims, those poor followers, or disciples, or whatever? They must be in shock."

"They are, I can assure you," said Pruden. "We've appealed to psychologists and psychiatrists in the city to help, and fortunately we found in the safe a surprisingly efficient list as to who contributed what, and how much, and so some of the money can be returned, and—"

"—but not their self-esteem or emotional health," Jan interrupted him to say.

"Or the nirvana they hoped for," added Pruden. "It's sad because apparently they were all so very *sincere*. All except Brother Robin."

Jan sighed. "I'm afraid there will always be candidates for a Guardian of Eden, we see it at the Settlement House too frequently. Just what Roger Gillespie said about the attraction of cults at Faber-Jones's party, remember? At least Brother Robin didn't plan to manufacture sarin and loose it in the subways."

Madame Karitska changed the subject by asking if Faber-Jones's daughter had been drugged. "Because he didn't say, and I didn't ask."

"Hadn't been there long enough, apparently, but she certainly seemed relieved to be out of it. Come to think of it," he added, "Faber-Jones, when he came for her, *did* tell me you'd given him the impression you had something to offer Laurie if she ever left the place."

"We'll see," she said noncommittally.

With a glance at his watch Pruden said, "Eight o'clock! We'll have to leave now, Jan's chaperoning a dance at the Settlement House and I'll have paperwork to do at head-quarters. But," he said, "I have news for you."

"Yes, tell her," Jan said, smiling.

"The chief finds himself extremely grateful to you for per-suading Amos Herzog to come out of retirement and help us—and I won't ask how," he added, although he longed to ask. "He's decided to swallow his stubborn pride and an-nounce publicly that the Trafton City Police Department now has a psychic as consultant. Acknowledgment at last! How about that?"

"I'm overwhelmed," she said dryly.

She did not have long to wait for another call from Faber-Jones; the next morning, in a surprisingly meek voice, he asked if he could make an appointment for his daughter to see her. "Because," he added, "you *did* say—admit it—that you had an idea how Laurie could find—as you phrased it—what she's looking for."

"Apparently I did, yes."

"She *hates* me," Faber-Jones said helplessly. "She's here with me now but won't talk, and since she wasn't away long enough to forfeit her room in the college dormitory she in-sists on returning there—to get away from me, I suspect—but has no intention of attending any classes. I've agreed to her moving there tonight, and to continuing her allowance, but only if she agrees to see you."

"Under duress, of course," said Madame Karitska lightly, and with a glance at her appointments the next day she suggested eleven o'clock the next morning. "But I'll see her on one condition, my friend."

"What?" he said eagerly.

"I'll tell you after I've seen her—at eleven o'clock tomorrow."

With a sigh Faber-Jones said, "I'll make sure she's out of bed by ten. And thank you."

The next morning, at only a few minutes after eleven, Madame Karitska opened the door to Faber-Jones's daughter, who hung back, looking sullen. She said, "My father sent me, I'm Laurie."

Madame Karitska smiled. "You mean he insisted, don't you?" and thought how very attractive the girl was, her long black hair tied back with what looked a shoestring, tall and slim in faded jeans and a white shirt and sneakers.

"Well," said Laurie defiantly, "he said either you or a psychiatrist, as if I've not seen enough of *them*. He said you told him—"

"Oh do come in, it's ridiculous our standing here," Madame Karitska told her.

The girl followed her into the living room, her glance swiftly running over the wall of books, the two couches facing each other across from the square coffee table. "He said you're a psychic," she told her. "Are you going to read my palm or something?"

How little they know each other, thought Madame Karitska,

and merely said, "Would you like tea or regular coffee or Turkish coffee? I'm simply a good friend of your father's, I'm fond of him, and I owe him my help."

"I don't need any help," the girl said curtly.

Madame Karitska smiled. "You were not very happy at the Guardians of Eden, were you? Or at college?"

She shrugged. "Okay, you win that round. I'll have Turkish."

"Turkish it is. And sit."

Madame Karitska took her time in the kitchen preparing the coffee, giving Laurie's hostility equal time to cool. When she returned it was to place the carafe on the table and sit down opposite her. "Have some if you'd like," she told her indifferently. "In the meantime, have you something small that you've worn for a long time?"

With a shrug the girl removed a ring from her finger. Ignoring the coffee she handed it across the table.

Madame Karitska held it, closed her eyes, and concentrated, waiting for the expected impressions of anger to diminish and something of character to surface. *Spoiled, rebellious, yes,* she thought, but there was also an impression that she had inherited one interesting trait from her father. Putting down the ring she said, "I believe you have a gift for organizing."

"Who, me?"

"Who else?"

Laurie shrugged. "Well, I guess at the commune I did—a little," she admitted. "I *liked* the commune."

"What did you organize?"

"Just the kids—sometimes. And a protest march; they left

it up to me, making the placards and signs, that kind of stuff."

Madame Karitska nodded. "And have you any plans as to what next?"

"I'm *not* going back to college," Laurie said defiantly.

"Then I wonder," said Madame Karitska, "if you'd give me ten days—no questions asked—ten days of your time to work at a job that's available."

"It's not baby-sitting, is it?" she said suspiciously, "because I said I liked kids?"

"I said no questions allowed," Madame Karitska reminded her.

Laurie sighed heavily. "Everybody wants to get into the act."

With a smile Madame Karitska said, "A pity, isn't it? Well—yes or no? Eight o'clock to five P.M. for ten days."

"Eight in the *morning* to five, are you kidding?"

"Yes or no?"

"How do I know if I'll like it?" demanded Laurie.

"Oh but you *won't* like it," Madame Karitska told her, startling her.

Laurie suddenly laughed. "I didn't expect *that*."

"I was being honest. You *won't* like it."

Laurie frowned. "Ten days, and then I can quit?"

"Of course. That would be the agreement."

Cautiously the girl said, "So where is this job, can you tell me that much?"

"Actually I'll show you where right now, but only if you agree, first, to those ten days of your time."

Laurie leaned over the table and poured thick Turkish coffee into a cup, took one sip, made a face and then, "Okay, if it's just ten days—like Russian roulette, isn't it? and I've nothing else to do."

Madame Karitska nodded. "Then I'll take you there now."

"All right, I've got my car."

"I saw it," said Madame Karitska, amused, a late-model convertible gleaming outside, and said gently, "I think it best that we walk."

Locking the door behind her, she and Laurie began their stroll down Eighth Street, neither of them speaking until they turned into Sixth Street to face the clusters of idle men along the sidewalks, smoking, tossing coins and talking; if they had learned to be polite to Madame Karitska, the sight of Laurie produced a volume of piercing whistles, to which Laurie said, "What the hell is this? Are you crazy, this *slum*?"

"Patience," said Madame Karitska, and guided her across the street to Help Save Tomorrow, where a truck had pulled up to the storefront and Daniel was unloading cartons of used toys and clothes.

"Daniel," said Madame Karitska, "this is Laurie, and she is going to spend ten days with you helping."

Laurie turned to look at her in astonishment. "Are you *serious*?"

Daniel smiled his broad friendly smile and said, "Never thought such a pretty girl would offer *help*. It's blessedly kind of you, miss."

Since Madame Karitska reached for a carton to carry into the store, Laurie had no choice but to grasp one of them and follow her. "If you think *this* is where I work for ten days you're mad."

"Quite mad," agreed Madame Karitska. "Careful with that carton, I see it has some china in it."

"But what does he do with all this . . . this junk?" she asked, shoving the carton onto the counter.

"Sell it for pennies or give it away," replied Madame Karitska. "You've arrived just in time to help unpack these cartons if you'd care to begin now."

"You really expect me to—" Cannily she stopped and said, "Would this count as one of the ten days? I mean, today's half over."

"Why not? He can certainly use you," and before Laurie could protest she said to Daniel, "Laurie's car is parked in front of my house. When you close at five o'clock would you mind walking her safely back to it?"

"My pleasure," Daniel said, beaming.

Madame Karitska, envisioning just how much would be left of a late-model convertible on Sixth Street said, "You'd better take a cab here in the morning, Laurie."

Daniel, slitting open a carton, shouted, "Man, look at this! A getting-married dress and nearly new! We're in luck *today*."

Trapped, Laurie accepted the bridal gown he'd thrust at her and said, "So what do I do with it?"

"Hangers over there," Daniel said, pointing, and Madame Karitska quickly left.

Once at home she put in a call to Faber-Jones at his office, and when she reached him she gave him her terms. "You recall there were conditions?"

He said eagerly, "You've seen her, then. All right, what are they?"

"For ten days no contact with her, my friend. She's consented to lend me ten days, and she has a job to do. No phone calls, no contact, no interference, no reminder of her previous life, you understand?"

"But that's horrible, Marina," he said, "I'll worry constantly."

"Let *me* do the worrying," she told him; as she would, even though she utterly trusted Daniel to look after her.

"But what on earth did you . . . well, prescribe for her?"

"Shock treatment," said Madame Karitska crisply, and hung up before he could ask more.

Nevertheless Madame Karitska could not help but wonder during the next days how this child of luxury would react to the challenge presented to her. She thought it possible that Laurie would keep her bargain, being a Faber-Jones, but nothing had been said about attitude, and eight hours at Help Save Tomorrow would be a challenge indeed, and yet . . . and yet . . .

Curiosity as well as concern had deepened by the fourth day of Laurie's indenture, and curiosity won. Madame Karitska walked over to Sixth Street and turned down it toward Help Save Tomorrow and stopped halfway down the street, startled by what she saw. Laurie was on top of a high stepladder outside Help Save Tomorrow with three teenaged boys below—skinheads, all of them—watching, laughing . . . taunting her? Laurie was hanging a sign over the store, a new one, and Madame Karitska stood very still, holding her breath, wondering if the boys were about to pull the ladder out from under Laurie—this was Sixth Street, after all—and then she realized they were not taunting her, they were steadying the ladder for Laurie. They were helping.

"Well, well," murmured Madame Karitska, and quickly retreated before she could be seen, and as she made her way back to Eighth Street she braced herself for her next appointment, which would not be an easy one.

She found Betsy Oliver already waiting for her in the hallway, her eyes red-rimmed. "I've just come from the funeral," she said. "Arthur's funeral."

Madame Karitska, unlocking the door, said, "I'm deeply sorry, Betsy, do come in. We'll talk, shall we?"

It was doubtful that Betsy even heard her; she walked into the living room and sat down on the couch and buried her face in her hands. "I feel so guilty, Madame Karitska, I feel just awful."

"Which is quite natural," she told her.

"Yes, but you've heard that he deliberately . . . I mean, he *wanted* to die? He'd still be alive if—"

This was going to be taxing, acknowledged Madame Karitska, and said, "Do you mean he'd be still alive if he'd not chosen to move to the Guardians of Eden, or still alive if you went with him? Which?"

"I think—" She stopped and blew her nose.

"Think what?"

Betsy said helplessly, "He must have been so lonely without us, me and Alice."

"Betsy, it was his choice to leave you and go, remember?"

"Yes, but he might—"

"Stop," said Madame Karitska sternly. "There is such a thing as fate, and there is such a thing as character. We each have our own destinies to work through; he had his, you have yours. Haven't you been happy lately?"

"B-but I feel so *guilty* at having been happy, while he—"

Madame Karitska firmly interrupted her. "How *is* it going, your artwork?"

Betsy said miserably, "Last week they hired me full-time—to sketch for Easter and birthdays and Valentine's—and I've been going two nights a week to the Trafton School of Art to— Oh, how can we *talk* about this at such a time!"

Madame Karitska smiled faintly. "Because you've been creating a very good life for yourself and your daughter."

"Yes, but Arthur—"

"Betsy, life *happens*. I, too, had a husband whose death was questionable. We had a very comfortable marriage and were relatively wealthy, or so I thought. I look back on it now with more perspective on how it ended."

"Ended," murmured Betsy, startled to hear something personal from her.

"Yes, he was killed in a car crash, and that, too, could have been deliberate, for he'd made some very foolish mistakes. I think he lacked the courage to tell me he was virtually bankrupt. He was an expert on diamonds, a diamond merchant, but *not* an expert on the stock market, or on options, in which he'd heavily invested without mentioning it to me at all. He invested not only carelessly but recklessly, and after my settling with his creditors there was almost no money at all. Only a handful of diamonds, very fine ones, fortunately. By selling them one by one, I managed to survive. When I arrived in this country and in Trafton I had just four diamonds left. And still have one," she added, not without humor. "But a certain perspective is needed about tragedies, Betsy, for they happen to nearly everyone. Eventually you have to learn, try to learn, that it's the eternal things that matter, and among them courage."

"But why?" demanded Betsy. "Why?"

"Because we're drawn to certain people, not always happily, and they to us, and not always by accident."

"What do you mean, 'not by accident'?"

"There are some philosophers—mystics," said Madame Karitska, "who believe that we choose our lives before we are born. To learn what has to be learned."

Betsy said desperately, "But what have I learned from Arthur except grief?"

"Well, for starters," she said lightly, "you've come in touch with your own self, you obeyed something deep inside of you, which was new for you: an uneasiness about Arthur and the Guardians of Eden that brought you to me. And later, in spite of his fury, you did something very, very difficult. You took a firm stand and said no to him. You've been growing up, Betsy," she said softly. "Think of it that way. And Alpha—Arthur—made *his* choice."

"But he made the *wrong* choice."

She nodded. "And that's what *he* learned. And there is nothing you can do except to mourn, accept, and make your own life without him."

"And Alice with no father," Betsy said sadly.

"He left *her*, too," she reminded her softly.

Betsy sighed and rose from the couch. "You can't really think we choose our lives?"

Madame Karitska smiled. "It helps one over the bad patches," she said lightly.

"I'll think about it," Betsy said. "Maybe I should read some books. At least I don't feel so . . . well, hysterical."

Madame Karitska said, "You may even stop hating yourself, given time."

Betsy nodded. "I do hate myself now, don't I."

"And the best antidote is your work, Betsy," she pointed out. "And I see you've let your blond hair grow long again, and it's lovely."

Betsy leaned over and kissed her on the cheek. "Thank you—and I don't feel *quite* so guilty now."

"Good," said Madame Karitska, and saw her to the door. It had been a long morning and there were two appointments still to come, and there had been a mysterious long-distance call, a secretary making an appointment, late the next week for a Mr. Smith, about which she felt uneasy. She was about to close her door when Kristan pounded down the stairs—his hiking boots were always noisy.

He said, "I read about it in the newspapers, she just left you, didn't she? Is she okay?"

"She will be," she told him.

"I just might give her a ride home," he said. "She had to sell their car, you know, she couldn't afford to keep it." He flew out of the front door and she heard him shouting to Betsy.

For anything to pry Kristan loose from his painting was certainly startling. For Madame Karitska this was the second surprise of her day—she *liked* surprises, and entered her apartment smiling.

13

The people who came and went on Eighth Street always interested Madame Karitska, and she soon became aware that a very attractive young woman had moved into one of Mrs. Chigi's unfurnished apartments diagonally across the street from her. The girl looked alive and interested in life and without pretension as she cheerfully carried groceries up the steps, usually in faded jeans, sneakers, and a sweatshirt, her long golden hair swept into a ponytail. Since nothing was completely private on Eighth Street, Kristan reported that her name was Kate and she was rumored to be a writer of some sort, doing research, or so her landlady believed, and had rented the two rooms on the second floor.

Her arrival on Eighth Street was only three weeks old when Madame Karitska responded to a knock on her door one morning and opened it to find her neighbor standing there.

"Hello," the girl said eagerly, "I'm Kate Margus and I'd like to make a two-hour appointment with you. Could you tell me how much you'd charge?"

A startled Madame Karitska said, "That's certainly unusual; may I ask why two hours?"

"Because I've just learned what the sign 'Readings' on your window means. I hear that you're a psychic, and a *good* one, and I'm hoping you can help me."

Both amused and curious Madame Karitska glanced at her watch. "I've forty-five minutes until my next client. Why don't you come inside—I won't charge you—and explain why a two-hour appointment." The girl was, after all, a neighbor, but two hours would be taxing indeed if she understood what psychometry entailed. As the girl followed her into the living room she said, "Neighborhood gossip reports that you're a writer?"

"Embryonic," she said. "I mean, I've had a few articles published, but . . ." Giving the wall of books a startled glance, as people so often did, she seated herself on a couch and said, "I guess I should first ask if you've heard of Charmian Cowper."

This was unexpected. Madame Karitska, about to offer coffee or tea, abruptly sat down. "Charmian Cowper! Good heavens yes!" she exclaimed. "Surely the most brilliant actress of our time—of *my* generation certainly, or even of the last century. She toured Europe when I lived there, I saw her twice on the stage. Unforgettable!"

Kate nodded. "She sang, too, in one of the few films she made. . . . Wonderful throaty voice. That's why I'm here."

Puzzled, Madame Karitska said, "Because of Charmian Cowper?"

The girl nodded. "She died in 1989 at the age of sixty-eight, only three months after her last performance as Lady Macbeth. And my mother, Ellen Margus, died a year and a half ago, and . . . and I inherited a small black trunk—"

"Trunk?" echoed Madame Karitska, thoroughly mystified now.

"Yes, and in my mother's will . . ." Here she burrowed into a pocket and brought out a slip of paper. "In my mother's will she left me—and I quote—'a trunk that *I* inherited—as you will now, my dear—and on the interior of the lid inside I've glued an envelope explaining from whom *I* inherited it. You'll find the key to the trunk in the china cookie jar in my kitchen. I believe you will find its contents of interest, and since I can leave you so little money I feel a few of the objects can be sold now. With discretion.' "

Thoroughly puzzled now Madame Karitska said, "And what did you find?"

"I opened the trunk and in the envelope was a copy of Charmian Cowper's will, sent to my mother by Charmian Cowper's lawyer following her death, and bequeathing the trunk to her oldest and dearest friend Ellen Winston Margus—that's my mother," she explained, " 'with love and gratitude.' "

"What a treasure," murmured Madame Karitska.

With a mingling of anger and passion the girl said, "But my mother never told me—never *mentioned*—that she ever knew Charmian Cowper, and it sounds as if they knew each other since childhood. I mean, anyone else would have *loved* to brag about knowing such a celebrity, but my mother never mentioned it, not ever, even to me."

Finding this strange, too, Madame Karitska only nodded and waited.

"Now I want—having adored her in films, and now *this*—I want to write her biography; I have to, I must, it's why I've taken a year off from my very good job in advertising, and why I've moved to Eighth Street before I run out of money doing research. I mean, here is this trunkful of old playbills and photographs, a few costumes, a gorgeous fan, a rather odd necklace, and I find I don't know what any of them mean. Or meant to *her*. There's never been a real biography written— lots of articles about her work, yes, but nothing of her personal life, and all I find are *facts*. She was always so private, you know, and my landlady said you can pick up feelings and reactions from holding things, and receive impressions?"

Madame Karitska said with relief, "At last I begin to understand."

"Yes, and I so hope— But not even the facts agree. All the movie magazines say she was born in Hungary in 1923, *Who's Who in America* says she was born in Austria in 1922, but her obituary said she was born in Hopetown, Pennsylvania, in 1921."

"In America! In Pennsylvania!" exclaimed Madame Karitska, remembering an exotic and inexplicably European charm.

"Yes," said Kate, and added pointedly, "And my mother was also born in Hopetown in 1921."

This met with a startled silence, until, "You've begun to interest me very much," admitted Madame Karitska. "I enjoy mysteries—"

"It's more like detective work," sighed Kate. "Also expensive. I've made two trips to Hopetown, and spent a small

fortune on movie magazines; did you know they're considered collectors' items now? except I also found some in flea
markets, mercifully. Did you know Charmian Cowper married four times?"

"No, I had no idea—*four* times?"

"Yes, and not until she was thirty years old, and then
to a director thirty years older than she was. She was so beautiful and magnetic, there could—*must?*—have been love
affairs, don't you think?" Returning to the practical she
brought out a memo pad. "I've made notes about her husbands; I'll leave these with you. I looked them all up, it
needed a whole month and wasn't easy . . . movie magazines
again."

"You *have* been busy," agreed Madame Karitska.

"Then when—I mean, may I make an appointment for
two hours with you? I can bring some of my mother's things
over here; I've several boxes of *hers*, but I don't quite know
how to get the trunk here."

Madame Karitska smiled. "It might be much simpler if I
come to your trunk."

"Oh, would you?" she said eagerly. "My place is still a
mess. . . . And you must call me Kate. I'm in apartment number two-oh-two. When are you free?"

Madame Karitska walked over to her desk to her appointment calendar. Some of her clients came in once a month,
some twice a month, others she never saw again, but definitely there was a welcome block of time tomorrow. She had
planned to visit her favorite thrift shop uptown, hoping that

an old Chanel suit there was still in good repair, but definitely Charmian Cowper and Kate were proving far more interesting than Chanel.

"Tomorrow," she said, "from one o'clock to three?"

Kate looked radiant. "Wonderful," she said. "I can't wait to see what we can learn."

Madame Karitska, watching this exuberant child leave, found that she, too, could scarcely wait to see what might be learned.

The next afternoon, a few minutes before one o'clock, Madame Karitska was buzzed through the front door of the apartment house where Kate lived. She was waiting for her at the top of the stairs. "I've gotten organized," she told her, "I've been so busy researching Charmian that my mother's personal papers remained in storage until yesterday. My furniture's *still* there, as you can see," she added, pointing toward a room furnished with only three filing cabinets, a computer, a typewriter, a desk and a small trunk, and, in a corner, a card table heaped with magazines and a box, with two straight chairs pulled up to it. "I thought—for your visit—I should pin that photo of Charmian on the wall; I bought it in New York. To inspire."

Madame Karitska had already noticed it on arrival, for it dominated the room, a large glossy photograph with the remembered bone structure of the face, the subtle slant of her almond-shaped eyes with a hint of sadness lurking in them, and that passionate mouth that a million men had longed to kiss. . . . Yet how those eyes could flash, she remembered, and the lips part in a radiant smile.

"Tell me about your visit to Hopetown," suggested Madame Karitska, "since you feel that's where your mother knew Charmian. Did you learn—"

"A lot about very little," quipped Kate. "I spent four days searching through court records. No listing of any Charmian Cowper among the birth records for 1921. I found in the local library some very old 1928-to-1930 directories, and my grandparents were listed there, but no Cowpers. I couldn't even find the two-family house where my mother grew up; it's become a mall now, full of stores and restaurants."

"A long time ago," Madame Karitska reminded her, and added thoughtfully, "the thirties would have been Depression years. . . ."

Kate nodded. "I realized that when I remembered what my mother told me about my grandfather. I never met him . . . he was a minister, and Mother said rather tartly that he gave half his money to the poor, and intentionally lived in a poor neighborhood—positively saintlike, but a bit frustrating for my mother. My last bit of research before I left was to visit the Historical Room at the Hopetown library. I xeroxed the first two pages of each 1930 through 1931 newspaper—it was only a weekly in those days—and I included an old map."

She placed the map on the table and they each sat down in a folding chair and she spread out the map. "I've circled where my mother grew up at 124 Speedway Avenue." She grinned. "My mother used to call the street a Speedway to

Oblivion, but it *has* to be where she knew Charmian Cowper, darn it. My mother lived there until she went off to college."

"And what's this?" asked Madame Karitska, pointing to a large blank circle adjoining Speedway Avenue.

Kate referred to her notes. "It was a swamp until they filled it in; during the Depression they called it Camp Town. Before that—probably before any bankers ended up broke and retreated there—it was known as Shanty Town."

"If no Cowpers were listed in the city directories they could have been renters and not listed," pointed out Madame Karitska. "What do you have there?"

"Photos of Charmian's husbands. One, the director whom she first married, Vladimir Mirkov, and very distinguished, as you can see: white hair and goatee. Unfortunately he died five years later. Next the two Pretty Men—that's what I call them—very young actors, Hayden Marsh and Peter Hastings, but each of those marriages lasted only about a year, and then *much* later came Dr. Ralph Palmer, a cardiologist. Since she died of a heart attack, she may have met him because she went to him for treatment when she began to have trouble." She handed the photographs to Madame Karitska. "She must have touched them, fingered them, can you pick up any hints of how she felt, any impressions?"

Madame Karitska reached for the photograph of the first husband, Vladimir Mirkov, and became very still, her eyes closed as she concentrated until, soon, she was filled with a deep sense of sadness.

"What is it?" asked Kate anxiously.

"She didn't love him," said Madame Karitska, frowning. "Something very poignant had happened to her before this marriage when she was thirty, there is a vivid impression of her turning to this older man, this friend, for comfort. A sense of great loss haunted her; I'd guess that he accepted the little she offered and was grateful."

"How awful," Kate said soberly. "Then we must try the earlier years, go back to—"

Madame Karitska nodded. "—to before she married without love at thirty? This is your mother's box of personal papers?"

Kate reached over and lifted off its cover for her. "Feel free to explore, I've not had any real time to do that."

It was not a large box, roughly sixteen inches by ten inches, and Madame Karitska first drew out a thick collection of Christmas cards bound in yellow ribbon. Untying the ribbon she spread them out on the table. There were no envelopes. As she opened one of them a faint scent of flowers assailed her nostrils; there was no signature inside, only a large *K* scrawled under the usual "Happy Holidays." Opening each card—and there were at least twenty of them—she met with the same signature of *K* and the same remnants of what had been a dried flower. "I can identify this fragrance," she said. "It's the herb rosemary taped inside each card," and glancing at Kate she added, " 'Rosemary for Remembrance.' "

"It couldn't be my father, his name was Charles. How mysterious—and who is *K*?"

"A pity the envelopes are missing. What's that you have from the Cowper trunk?"

"Passports, old ones," and Kate handed three of them to her. "There's also a book of Emily Dickinson's poetry, a battered old doll, a gorgeous medieval gown of brocade from one of her Shakespeare plays, and under it—" She glanced at Madame Karitska and stopped. "What has startled you?"

"This passport," she told Kate. "In 1939 Charmian Cowper made a trip abroad, and to Poland, of all places, a dangerous place to visit in 1939 when Hitler was about to invade the country. And if you're accurate about her being born in 1921 she'd have been only eighteen years old."

"You're kidding," said Kate, and frowned. "I know she was 'discovered' at fifteen, singing in a crummy New York café while going to acting school, but 1939?" Consulting her notes she added, "She made her famous Broadway debut when she was seventeen, in *Romeo and Juliet*, and the critics went crazy over her Juliet. How could she have gone to Europe when still playing Juliet?"

Turning a page of the passport Madame Karitska said, "One might also ask how she got there in such a troubled year. According to this she was there only two weeks and returned to America two weeks later; there's a reentry stamp here." Frowning over this, "Did she go for publicity? The offer of a role in a new play? If so, the political situation in Poland in 1939 would have quickly dissuaded her. And," she said, startled, "she visited Poland *again* in 1945—just after the war."

"More mystery," sighed Kate. "Let's see if any explanations can be found here," and delving into the trunk, "Here are playbills. She was Ophelia in *Hamlet*, Portia in *Julius Caesar*,

Rosalind in *As You Like It*, Katherine in *Taming of the Shrew* . . .
and after that a Noël Coward play, and there are the three
films, *The Duchess Misbehaves, Song of Love*—that's where
she sang—and *Wild Is the Night*. What are you finding?"

"This," said Madame Karitska, bringing from Kate's mother's
box a snapshot of five children squeezing themselves into a
line and obviously giggling. "A very old photograph, and
somewhat faded," she said, remembering ancient Kodak
cameras, but she held it close for a moment, not sharing it
yet, her glance drawn to the child second in the line: a ragged
dress, a smudge of dirt on her cheek, her hair a tangle of black
curls.

This could have been me as a child, she thought, *unwashed,
ragged, a beggar child*. The boy at the end of the line looked
equally shabby; the two were a contrast to the others.

"There's writing on the back of that," said Kate, pointing.

Madame Karitska turned it over to read in a childish scrawl,
"Me, Kitta Sinka, Gert Brown, Betsy Palmer, Jai Kostich."
*Then Kitta was the ragged child, and why does she look famil-
iar*, she wondered, *because she reminds me of myself, or . . . ?*
To Kate she said, "There are two 'K's here, a Kitta and a Kos-
tich." and she handed Kate the snapshot without comment.

"Isn't she darling!" exclaimed Kate. "That's my mother on
the left, the little blond girl . . . but what company she kept!
Are those two," she said, pointing, "from Camp Town, do you
suppose? I've a 1931 news clip from the *Hopetown Bugle*
about Camptown, and how they were finally trying to clear it
of squatters. No doubt for a mall," she added with humor.

"I think we should see that clipping," Madame Karitska told her.

Kate nodded. "I'll dig it out in a minute but first I want you to see this necklace; it caught my eye right away when I opened the trunk for the first time. I even took it to a jeweler here in Trafton to evaluate, it's so unusual."

She held it up to admire. Hanging from a long gold chain was a heart-shaped turquoise-colored stone in which five tiny gold stars had been set, the turquoise framed by a hammered-gold heart-shaped frame, from which were suspended three gold coins.

"Unusual, yes!" agreed Madame Karitska.

"The jeweler said the coins are Austrian, and twenty-four-carat gold, but he hadn't the slightest idea what the turquoise heart was made of; he'd never seen anything like it and offered to send it to Sotheby's in Manhattan, hoping they could identify it, because it isn't a turquoise at all. Here," she said, and handed it to Madame Karitska.

Grasping it, at once Madame Karitska felt a shock. "Oh!" she said, and then, "Oh dear."

"What?" asked Kate. "You look weird, what is it?"

Catching her breath she told her shakily, "There's no need to concentrate on this, it's all here, and all at once . . . that passion you looked for, Kate. And grief. And the love of soul mates. Dear God, yes, the love."

An awed Kate stared at her. "She did love, then, and was loved?"

"By whomever gave this to her, yes."

Kate said in a whisper, "The lawyer—he wrote later that she was wearing this when she died."

"I think it was always with her, and *years* before her death."

"I'm so glad," Kate said simply. "I don't mean that she died, but she gave so much, affected so many, I'm so glad she had . . . except that's why . . ." She reached for the book of Emily Dickinson poems. "She underlined one of these poems," she said, handing it to her. "I so wonder what happened to them, and I did wonder why this particular poem. I'll find the news clipping about Camp Town that you want," and she crossed the room to her folder of sorted papers.

But Madame Karitska, with a glance at her watch, said, "Kate, I really must leave now, you've not noticed the time."

"But, oh how sad!" she complained.

"Do you mind if I take the book of poems with me? If you come at four o'clock I'll brew Turkish coffee and we can continue this." And with a wave of her hand she hurried down the stairs and crossed the street to find her three o'clock client waiting impatiently for her at the door, a plain little round-faced woman clutching her tweed jacket. With apologies she unlocked her door, and if she had feared that any impressions might be overshadowed by her thoughts of a glamorous Charmian Cowper the tears in this woman's eyes at once captured her full attention. "Do come in, give me a minute to reheat some coffee for you, you look as if you could use it. You're Madeline, aren't you?"

"Yes. And thank you," and while Madame Karitska headed for the kitchen Madeline seated herself on the couch.

"You do know how I work," she called from the kitchen. "I
need something of yours that you've worn a long time."

"My wristwatch," Madeline told her, and once she reap-
peared she handed it to Madame Karitska and accepted the
cup of coffee with eagerness.

Holding the wristwatch, concentrating with closed eyes,
she said, "I feel that you're under much tension and it's reflected in your lower back, which is causing you much pain."

"That's for sure," Madeline said, sipping her coffee.

"And," continued Madame Karitska, "you've a very important decision to make, and I will be frank with you; I cannot
say whether it was in the past or ahead of you—past and future can often blur—but it has something to do with your
husband . . . his first initial is M?"

"Yes," she said, startled.

". . . and he is in some sort of legal situation that has separated you—by your choice. So much tension! You are in
doubt whether to join him or not; you are each living alone?"

The woman nodded miserably. "I don't know *what* to do."

"You have recently spent much time in a courtroom," continued Madame Karitska. "That's very clear. And now he is
far away. Do you love him?"

Madeline nodded. "Oh yes . . . it's just—you see, I've always lived in Trafton, I grew up here, all my friends are here,
even my mother. I don't like change but suddenly everything's changed, even his name."

Ah, thought Madame Karitska, sensing the meaning of the
courtroom. "He was testifying, am I right?"

Madeline nodded.

Witness protection, thought Madame Karitska, but to query this might frighten her, and she was already in a state of terror at leaving Trafton. She said gently, "You have to choose, don't you."

"Yes. Can't you tell me? It's why I came to you, I hoped you'd help me choose."

Madame Karitska felt a stab of pity. "No one can help you with such a choice," she told her. "It's up to you . . . two very clearly defined paths lie before you."

"Yes, but—"

Very gently Madame Karitska said, "Try to picture those two paths, neither of them easy. Which do you feel is the greater sacrifice? Your husband, or your friends and family here? Try." And thinking with some humor that this was a day for poetry, she closed her eyes again and recited from memory two verses of a favorite poem. " 'Two roads diverged in a yellow wood, and sorry I could not travel both and be one traveler, long I stood and looked down one as far as I could to where it bent in the undergrowth,' " and skipping to the last verse, " 'I shall be telling this with a sigh somewhere ages and ages hence; two roads diverged in a wood, and I—I took the one less travelled by, and that has made all the difference.' "

There was a long silence and then Madeline said, "So I'm not the only one to— that was beautiful, was it a poem?"

"Yes, by Robert Frost."

"I'd like a copy of that," she said eagerly. "Maybe if I read it again and again I might dare—not be so frightened."

Madame Karitska rose and walked to her bookcase and drew out a paperback volume of poems. "If it moved you, as I think it did, take this with you, you'll find the poem there." She opened the book to "The Road Not Taken." "As a gift. In fact," she said with a smile, "he may be of more help to you than I. For there's always choice, you know. Limited by character and your history and personality, but always there's choice."

Madeline suddenly smiled at her, astonishingly pretty when she smiled, and opening her purse she counted out Madame Karitska's fee. "Thank you—ever so much," she told her, and walked to the door, opened it, and was gone.

And I will never know, thought Madame Karitska, amused, *but I think—I dare to think she'll open herself up to adventure, and a move.*

But it was nearly time for Kate to join her, and at last she could return to the poetry book found in Charmian Cowper's trunk. Opening it she was not surprised at what she found: she was already beginning to guess, very slowly, where they were heading, and what they would find; she had outlined the exquisite and heartrending poem:

> *I measure every grief I meet*
> *With analytic eyes;*
> *I wonder if it weighs like mine,*
> *Or has an easier size.*
>
> *I wonder if they bore it long,*
> *Or did it just begin?*

I could not tell the date of mine,
It feels so old a pain.

I wonder if it hurts to live,
And if they have to try,
And whether, could they choose between,
They would not rather die.

She sat quietly, allowing the pain of the words to flow through her, and then she noted that further along in the book a page had been marked by a bookmark, and turning to it she discovered a snapshot, faded and familiar. She had just turned it over when Kate knocked on the door.

"Kate?" she called. "Come in . . . Kate . . ."

Opening the door Kate said, "What is it?"

"I've a surprise for you; come and see what I've found, and *not* from your mother's box, but from Charmian Cowper's trunk."

It was the same snapshot of five children in a row; turning it over a different hand had written, "Ellen, me, Gert Brown, Betsy Palmer, Jai," all with a child's flourish of decorations: musical notes, figures of angels and of tiny faces.

"The two match," breathed Kate in astonishment.

"Yes, and the 'me' in this one is Kitta Sinka."

Kate scowling over this, said, "What can it mean? My mother knew this Kitta Sinka, she also knew Charmian Cowper, but these two photographs—"

"I think," said Madame Karitska, "that I'd like to see the news clipping now that you brought me."

"Why? You're sensing something important, aren't you."

Madame Karitska nodded. "Gypsies." And scanning the news clipping she read aloud, " 'Too many of the squatters are gypsies and they have to *go*. There have been complaints from local residents of nefarious fortune-telling schemes, and Police Chief Higgins strongly suspects they may be behind the recent robberies on Mountain Avenue, and it is the considered opinion—' " She stopped. "And so they were forced to go. In 1931."

"How cruel," said Kate. "In the movies gypsies are so *glamorous*."

"A typical Hollywood misconception," said Madame Karitska, "they're still being run out of towns in Europe."

"But what is the connection?" cried Kate. "What is the *secret*? The one my mother kept all those years."

Madame Karitska smiled forgivingly. "You're clinging to preconceived notions, Kate. Charmian Cowper is—was—Kitta Sinka—a gypsy, as was the boy Jai, I'm sure—which means that at the age of eleven she left Hopetown, her family scattered, and at fifteen she was singing in that 'crummy' café that publicists have described, but singing as Charmian Cowper, and only your mother knew the truth and concealed it. And for this Kitta was eternally grateful."

"But why?" asked Kate, frowning.

"My dear," said Madame Karitska, "you have to have belonged to a minority race to understand how things were in those days, perhaps even worse than today, but particularly in a town like Hopetown. There are always prejudices; they seem always with us, they simply change color and history and identity from decade to decade. But gypsies remain anathema in many countries."

"But Jai, the boy Jai Kostich, was he a gypsy, too?"

"She loved him."

"You mean he's the one—"

"Definitely, I feel it. *Definitely.* And if she was being 'discovered' at the age of fifteen she must have already been separated from him by circumstances."

"I wonder why . . . and how."

Madame Karitska sighed. "I'm thinking of those mysterious—possibly frantic—trips to Poland that she made, Kate. There must be records, possibly not, and she can no longer tell us. If they scattered and went to Poland—"

"*Poland!*" gasped Kate.

"It wouldn't have been a fortunate choice, Kate, for it wasn't only Jews who were being sent to the concentration camps; half a million gypsies ended up in the ovens, and in Poland they were sent to Dachau. In 1939."

Kate's head jerked up in shock. "In 1939?"

Madame Karitska nodded. "I think she traveled—somehow—to Poland in 1939 to look for Jai. Whom she loved."

"Oh God," murmured Kate. "And didn't find him?"

"And again when the war was over, and she was twenty-five."

"And still missing!"

"And five years later married her director Vladimir Mirkov."

"With a broken heart," whispered Kate.

"And that's the secret your mother kept—out of love for her. And out of love for her and her loyalty, Kitta Sinka sent your mother every year a Christmas card with a sprig of rosemary."

"For remembrance," said Kate, still stricken. "But it's so *sad*," she cried. "The only man she loved! And so passionately, so completely."

"And yet . . ." began Madame Karitska, "and yet . . ."

"Yet what?"

"How would you have ended the story?"

Kate said, "Why, by—" She stopped frowning.

Madame Karitska nodded. "I don't think they ever lost each other, I like to believe so—but he could never have been confined to *her* world, and if she remained Kitta Sinka just think of what the world—all of us—would have lost . . . and do you think she could have left audiences of thousands in tears, when she played tragedies, if she'd not experienced devastating loss herself? But they *loved* . . . and if you understand that, as well as your mother so lovingly protecting her all those years, you will understand the real mystery of Charmian Cowper. And of love."

"I only feel like crying," admitted Kate.

Madame Karitska smiled and rose. "Then it's time I brewed that Turkish coffee that I promised you. You'll find it very potent and distracting." Hearing a knock on her door she added, "Mind seeing who that is, Kate? I'm not expecting any client."

Busy in the kitchen, she heard Jenny call to her, "It's a young man delivering flowers to you."

Not Amos again, thought Madame Karitska, and leaving the coffee to brew she walked back into the living room, to find a familiar young man holding an enormous bouquet of flowers for her. "John!" she exclaimed. "John Painter!"

He grinned at her. "You once introduced me to the police as Miroslav Khudoznik, the Russian word for painter being Khudoznik, remember? Or so you said. Or shouldn't I remind you of my indiscretions . . . Am I interupting something? I brought you flowers because my recording, 'Once in Old Atlantis,' has gone gold. Sold so many I'm not just Top Ten but I've a gold record—and I owe it to— Who are *you?*" he asked Kate abruptly.

"Kate, this is John Painter—"

"Oh, I knew that at *once*," said Kate. "I'm Kate Margus."

"Kate," said Madame Karitska, opening a cabinet in search of a vase, "is writing a biography of Charmian Cowper, and I've been helping her to identify a few items from Miss Cowper's trunk, which she inherited."

"You knew her?" gasped Painter. "No, you couldn't have, you're too young. How on earth did you inherit a trunk of hers?"

"My mother," Kate told him proudly. "She was a wonderful singer, too, wasn't she? You've heard her?"

"These are gorgeous flowers," Madame Karitska told him, "but you've brought me so many I shall have to divide them and use two vases."

But John Painter wasn't listening. "*Heard* Charmian Cowper? I idolize that woman. What's more," he told Kate, "I've the pleasure of owning a recording of her singing 'Night of Love,' and 'Gypsy's Lament.' "

"But she didn't make any recordings," said Jenny firmly. "I'd have known, I really would, because I've been doing research on her for weeks and weeks."

He laughed. "Obviously you don't know how devious we fans can be. What I own is a bootleg recording that was sneakily recorded at one of her 1972 concerts in Scandinavia, one of the very few she gave. No, I didn't record it, but one of the fun things about money—having it, I mean—is that I bought it for a small fortune. The sound is a little muffled, but believe me, she's still great. Like to hear it?" He turned to Madame Karitska. "You, too? I could bring it here, or you could come to my studio apartment."

"I'd love to hear it," said Kate breathlessly. "An actual recording! Bliss."

Madame Karitska smiled at them over the bouquet of flowers she was arranging in a vase, and recklessly told them a lie. "Take Kate with you," she told him. "I've a client coming soon, and after all, it's Kate who is writing her biography."

"Want to come now?" asked John Painter of Kate.

"Love to."

They were regarding each other with more than casual interest, which intrigued her.

"Do you have a title for the biography yet?" he asked Kate.

She looked at Madame Karitska and smiled. "I'm thinking of calling it *Charmian Cowper: The Story of Kitta Sinka*."

"You'll have to explain *that* to me," he told her, and with a nod and a smile and a wink for Madame Karitska he escorted Kate out of the room and they were gone, leaving behind a scent of flowers and a deflation of the electricity that had flowed between the two upon meeting.

14

Madame Karitska had hesitated for a long time to establish fees for her work. Being new on Eighth Street, and unknown for a number of weeks, she had charged very little, often leaving it up to her clients to contribute what they could afford. Now that her readings had multiplied, and her reputation expanded beyond Eighth Street, many of her clients were prosperous, and some she found downright frivolous, wanting only to ask when they were going to meet that wonderful man they would marry, and with whom they would live happily forever after. In their case she wished she could send them to the carnival out in the Edgerton section, where a fortune-teller would tell them exactly what they wanted to hear, but this was Eighth Street, not Cavendish Square, and she kept her fees modest and her readings honest, refusing to look too far into the future unless she foresaw danger. This was not only out of principle but because it needed more than psychometry; it needed an almost trancelike state that was depleting. She preferred to decipher the past and the present, and frankly told her clients so.

"Because," as she explained, not entirely truthfully, "what you do with *now* creates your future," which at least encouraged them to wake up to a life they were all too often moving through like sleepwalkers.

Waking on Monday morning, Madame Karitska considered her schedule for this day with unusual curiousity. At ten o'clock she would meet the mysterious Mr. Smith—in her experience almost everyone who gave the name of Smith was not really a Smith—and in late afternoon she planned to visit Help Save Tomorrow, since at noon tomorrow Laurie Faber-Jones would have completed her tenth day of enforced labor at the shop with Daniel. She wondered if Laurie would be ready at last to return to college, or at the very least understand that she had lived a very privileged life and that it was time for her to regard it with a shade more humility. Obviously Daniel had taken good care of her; the three boys had *not* tipped over her ladder when she was hanging the sign— Daniel would have seen to that—but other than hanging a sign Laurie could very well have spent most of the ten days reading a book in a corner and sulking. There was no way of knowing, and she had resisted any further strolls to Sixth Street to observe.

Promptly at ten o'clock there was a firm knock on her door, and Madame Karitska prepared herself to meet Mr. Smith, but a surprise awaited her. Opening the door she found a familiar figure standing there and exclaimed, "Roger Gillespie! *You're* Mr. Smith?"

"My secretary was playful," he said, smiling. "May I come in?"

"Of course—in fact, welcome," she told him, not believing at all that it was his secretary who had been playful.

Once inside he closed the door firmly behind him, saying, "I've not forgotten—startled as I was—how you retrieved a scene from my past simply by holding a piece of shrapnel, and it's occurred to us that possibly your talent may be useful. We badly need some help that we hope you can give us, help that could save us invaluable time and research."

"If I can, I'd be happy to," she said, curious to say the least, and invited him to leave his guardlike stance by the door and move to a couch. "You've been well?" she asked, as he sat down and placed a briefcase on the coffee table. To ease the tension that he'd brought with him into the room she added, "I've just made a pot of coffee. Cream or sugar?"

"Black," he said absently, zipping open his briefcase.

She placed the carafe on the table with two cups, sat down opposite him, folded her hands and waited.

With a frown he said, "I can only hope you remember something of the worries I described at Mr. Faber-Jones's party?"

"Vividly," she responded.

"Good. It saves so much time." Placing a sheaf of papers on the table he explained, "I have here the resignations, or similar documents, from eleven very talented men who for years had worked with long-established electronic firms but have resigned, presumably to start their own companies."

"And you think one of them ... You spoke of 'rogue' geniuses?"

"Yes," he said. "I'll be frank. We've assumed that our

mischief makers, if we're correct, would situate themselves as far from cities as possible—and from us," he added dryly. "We've been combing the Midwest, a lot of small towns there, and the public-service companies—those people who send your monthly bills—have been served notice to report any unusually high electric bills."

"*Electric?*"

He said wryly, "Ironically, they would need an abnormal amount of power to build a machine that could, in turn, wipe out a nation's electricity."

"Ironic, yes," she agreed, still not understanding what he had in mind for her.

He drew one sheet of paper from the table, and eyeing her closely handed it to her. "This man—I won't use the names of any corporations—was a top man, one of their so-called geniuses." He handed it to her. "From only a signature can you tell me anything? Otherwise there's no hope of your aid."

Placing her hand on the signature she closed her eyes. "What a strange mind," she murmured, "full of such strange words . . . circuits, databases, PCs . . ." Without further comment she concentrated on deeper impressions reaching her. A brilliant man . . . sad about leaving . . . She opened her eyes. "But he is very ill; I've not read his letter but—oh, *very* ill, and—"

"No need," he told her, and for the first time smiled. "I was testing you. My apologies; *very* ill, in fact since then he has unfortunately died." He reached for the carafe of coffee and poured himself a cup. "Shall we get down to business now?"

She looked at him and laughed. "Very foxy, Mr. Gillespie."

He did not smile. "I have to say that I'm deeply relieved that signatures alone can speak." Becoming professional again he continued. "We decided to go no farther back than two years, so I hand you eleven letters—"

"Two years!" she exclaimed.

He nodded. "We had to set a limit to our queries, which have taken months to collect and assimilate. It also needed a great deal of time to capture the *original* signatures, rather than machine copies." He frowned. "Perhaps I was thinking of you even then, having realized that copies are never the same as originals."

"No," she said, taking the sheaf of papers he handed to her.

He gestured toward what he had given her and said ruefully, "What I've just handed you are the signatures of eleven men with IQs of probably two hundred, or possibly the intelligent quotient would slide off the charts completely. There have been others, but we were able to trace them satisfactorily. These eleven supposedly left to start their own electronic companies, with names of"—referring to his notes—"names of Pockets, Splash, HiTech, Dazzle, CoCo, and other improbable names. And to learn this much," he added, "my men had to haunt innumerable bars to strike up conversations with men or women who had worked with these eleven. But so far none of those companies has gone public, been listed on any stock exchanges, here or abroad, or been heard of by my friends, which we find of interest."

Puzzled, she asked, "But surely there were home addresses?

You made no effort to find and approach and interview these people?"

He sighed. "My suspicions of this," he said, nodding toward the papers in her lap, "used to be simply a gut feeling, because of my concern—and for some years—of the government's complacency in this area: our growing dependency on electricity, so ripe for terrorism, and terrorism is my business. But during the past two years it's become far more than a gut feeling, due to sources I can't name. Yet nobody's interested except my department. Or open to it. Or considers it possible. If we personally visited and interviewed each of these men . . ." He shook his head. "Disaster. They're no fools; I'd lose them. The one man—or men—we're looking for would go underground."

She smiled faintly. "So you operate on rumors, theories, suspicions, imagination, and intelligence of your own." Which, she decided, made him undoubtedly a genius, too. "You really believe in this."

"Oh yes."

"And what do you hope from me?"

He sighed. "I don't know. . . . What peculiarities or obsessions does a genius lock in his brain that might show up in a signature?"

She nodded. "Then let's start, shall we? So long as these are the original signatures. Have some coffee, this will take time."

Concentrating deeply on the first signed letter she closed her eyes and frowned. "Toys," she said. "*Toys?* This man is very excited, very certain; I see drawings of toys, very technical ones, games I think—on a computer? Are there such things?"

"Video games, yes," and with a glance at his notes Gillespie said, "Possibly this is the man who told friends his new firm would be called CoCo. Go on."

Removing the second letter she held it and after a few minutes smiled. "I don't feel this is your man, he's too serene. A very spiritual man, I think, quite dreamy and absentminded except in his work."

"That sounds innocuous—for the moment. Go on."

"Letter number three?" Eyes closed she said at last, "This man—oh *very* ambitious. Angry, too. Really, a handwriting analyst would have told you this at once . . . and full of resentment. An angry, brilliant man. It could be he."

Gillespie nodded. "His letter of resignation is certainly brief and very curt. Whatever he planned hasn't materialized— not yet at least. I'll check-mark him. Go on."

"Letter number four," she said. "This man—I gain a very distinct impression that he's an independent sort of man, bored with authority, determined to be on his own, as if the company's grown too big for him now. No other impressions."

"But another possibility," concluded Gillespie. "Try number five."

Madame Karitska nodded, and placed her hands on the signature of number five, and felt a jolt.

"What is it?" demanded Gillespie. "Are you ill?"

"This . . . this one," she faltered. "How astonishing! This one is familiar; this one I've 'felt' before."

"What do you mean, 'felt before'?"

"Here, in this room. A brilliant, half-mad brilliance, and—"
She stopped and looked at Gillespie. "I'm sorry, it shocked me
then, it shocks me now. A certain maliciousness, destructive,
and certainly a genius, but—"

Gillespie said in a hard voice, "I think you'd better tell me
about this." He poured a cup of coffee and handed it to her.
"Drink it," he told her. "You've gone as white as the prover-
bial sheet."

She took a sip of coffee and nodded. "Sorry. Let's see,
it happened probably two months ago. It was a woman,
quite rude—and rich," she added, and lifted both hands
to press them against her temple. "There have been so
many since then; let me think." Slowly the memory of it
returned to her. "Her name was Anna, she very pointedly said
she'd not give her last name, she'd come in a taxi, which was
waiting for her. And what she'd come to ask me was . . . oh
yes, if her husband had met another woman, because she insisted they were very happily married but she so rarely saw
him."

When she hesitated, still trying to recall details, he said,
"She'd brought something of his you would work with?"

"A wristwatch, yes. Old, very shabby. And I experienced
this same shock."

"Go on."

"She kept telling me what a genius he was, and—yes, she
said that with two friends he was starting an electronic company." She frowned. "In any case, he came home so rarely she
was sure there had to be another woman."

"Keep thinking," Gillespie told her.

"You really think—"

"From your reaction, it's possible. Did she happen to mention where this company was being started? In Trafton, for instance?"

"Oh no." She frowned. "She did, yes . . . Maine. As she was about to leave she said she couldn't understand why it had to be Maine."

"Maine!"

"Yes . . . a small town," she said. "I wish I could remember the name she gave . . . Digby? Danby? Denby? Darby? I reassured her there was no other woman, it was his work that kept him away and she definitely said Maine."

"Or so he told her," murmured Gillespie, and in exasperation said, "We didn't think of Maine, damn it. She didn't give her last name?"

"Only her first name, Anna."

"Never mind, he'll be on our list. And the impression you received alarmed you?"

She nodded. "A mind that never stilled . . . feverish . . . an impression, too, of malice—and danger." She shivered. "As she opened her purse to pay me, a number of memos drifted to the floor. One of them was left behind, and in case she returned for it . . ." She rose and went to her bookcase. "It's still here. Strange," she said, looking it over, "it has a list very much like the one Tanya mentioned at the party. Firewood, kerosene lamps, candles . . ." She gave it to him.

He made notes in his memo pad before saying, "There are six more to go through."

For the next forty-five minutes she made comments on the impressions she received from the remaining letters of resignation. Only one in particular appeared to interest Gillespie: a man whose character did not equal his intelligence; he struck her as—she could only say that he was a born follower, his emotions immature.

"Which can happen with brilliant people," Gillespie said. "Beware of followers."

Madame Karitska, remembering Alpha Oliver, nodded, and noted that Gillespie double-checked this man in his list of possibilities.

"So," he said at last, leaning back on the couch. "You've been more helpful than you realize, or than I expected." He smiled his charming smile, relaxed now, even returning to his cup of coffee. "Coincidences always interest me, I imagine they do you, too."

She returned his smile. "You mean our meeting at Mr. Faber-Jones's party, your obvious skepticism about clairvoyance, and now this." She nodded. "There are sometimes meaningful coincidences that lead us to think—"

"Yes?"

She said lightly, "That meetings are not always by chance."

He smiled. "I see that you've read Jung."

"Yes," and they smiled at each other with understanding. "And what now?" she asked after a long pause.

He gathered up his letters and repacked his briefcase.

"What next? We begin again," he told her. "But in Maine now. It will take time, and I'm always understaffed; I've few men to spare to find and become acquainted with one small town in Maine, but you've certainly given us an important fresh lead, this man whose impressions so upset you. His name and address are on our list; we can begin at this end to trace him, as well as in Maine." He rose, briefcase in hand. "Send me your bill, please," and he gave her his business card. With a glance at the simplicity of her apartment he added with a smile, "And don't stint on your bill, we can afford it."

And with this he left, but leaving behind him the very pleasant sensation of a man with whom she had, for a moment, exchanged much more than words.

Later, as she strolled down the street toward Help Save Tomorrow she thought it appropriate for this day that at the corner kiosk selling newwpapers the headline in the *Trafton Times* read CALIFORNIA'S ELECTRICAL SYSTEM ON THE VERGE OF FAILURE. Overload, Gillespie would say, of this she had no doubt. More and more electricity needed, more and more people, inventions and companies using it with complacency.

But Laurie was her business just now. The shop, as she approached it, looked calm, no boys with shaved heads hanging about, no fights. Opening the door she found Laurie removing books from a carton and placing them carefully on the shelves of the bookcase. Seeing her, Laurie looked for a moment as if she couldn't remember who she was and then, "Oh—hi!" she said.

"Hi to you, too," said Madame Karitska. "I've stopped in to remind you that your ten days are up tomorrow morning, and you're released from our agreement."

"Really?" said Laurie, startled, and looked around her with a critical eye. "It's certainly needed tons of work and organizing. Actually . . . actually, I'm going to be staying awhile, Mrs. Karitska—I mean Madame Karitska. You see," she explained as if to a child, "there's so much to be *done*. We're going to paint the walls, they're so grubby, and we're talking about a story hour on Saturday mornings for the kids. And Daniel's great but he simply *doesn't* know style, or how to *display* what comes in. Or advertise, either. I've persuaded him to put an ad in the Trafton community newsletter, which is where he is now."

Struggling to adjust to this new and formidable Laurie, Madame Karitska said, "And you're contributing books, I see—of your own?"

"Oh no," Laurie told her gleefully, "I visited a bookstore uptown yesterday and begged, really begged—can you imagine?"

Madame Karitska tried to imagine and failed. "That's certainly clever of you," she managed.

Laurie looked at her and suddenly grinned. "Okay, you got me hooked, darn you. I hate like hell admitting you were right, but I'm really *good* at this."

"So I've noticed," said Madame Karitska, smiling, and looked down at the child tugging at Laurie's skirt.

The child was persistent. "Laurie, Daniel said—and you *promised*—"

Laurie nodded. "I know, Moesha, but you'll soon have my skirt off if you keep pulling at it." And to Madame Karitska, "She wants to see the going-to-church dress we set aside for her. If you'll excuse us . . . ?"

"Of course," said Madame Karitska and watched the two of them walk to the rear, where a curtain had been strung across the corner. Reaching for a ruffled pink dress Laurie and Moesha disappeared behind the curtain, and there followed a few giggles and a "Wow!"

She turned as Daniel walked into the store, closing the door behind him. "Well, Daniel," she said, "Laurie's just told me she's going to stay awhile."

Daniel placed the package he was carrying on the counter and looked at her with his wise eyes. "That's one smart girl, she has me dizzy with plans," he said, "but I think you smarter."

"Me?"

He nodded. "You bring me one girl with a frozen heart," he told her, chuckling, "and just see her now."

Once again he had surprised her. "A frozen heart," she repeated, moved by his words, and as she walked slowly home she thought, *how poetic and how right of Daniel.*

As for herself she could finally soothe Faber-Jones's wounded feelings by telling him, at last, where he could find his daughter and for this she was glad, because she had missed him, but she would have to gently prepare him for a shock.

The last event of this day was the sheaf of flowers left on her doorstep, wrapped in plastic. The card inserted read, *I trust you are still considering.* They were not the first that Amos Herzog had sent. Amused, she carried them inside and placed them in a vase of water.

15

That night, following Roger Gillespie's visit, Madame Karitska slept restlessly, and toward morning experienced a strange dream. In her mind she entered a large room furnished from wall to wall, and ceiling-high, with endless rows of what looked like switchboards that glistened with tiny lights and knobs; above these the ceiling was a network of shining wires. When she awoke she knew that it was an important dream, it had meaning and she trusted it, remembering other such dreams ... above all, the pathetic elderly couple heartbroken over the death of their granddaughter, Jan Cooper Hyer, who had been killed in a car accident on the way to the airport for her first trip to Europe. Only one shoe and her passport were intact, somehow escaping the flames of the burning car, the passport with its photograph of a lovely young blond woman. She had been killed; but why, then, had Madame Karitska dreamed night after night of that young woman in a barren room, helpless but alive? Pruden had fought her insistence that it was someone else—not Jan Cooper Hyer—in the wrecked car; Madame Karitska had set out to prove him wrong.

"Her grandparents mentioned that this young woman had

the sixth sense," she told Pruden. "I believe she walked into my dreams to send a message."

And ultimately they had found Jan Cooper Hyer in a barren warehouse, tied to a post, cold and hungry.

This dream of the night was no less vivid. This dream had to be connected with Roger Gillespie's visit; and this, then, was what he would find, if he was fortunate, but it was of no use to him, of course, since it gave no hint of its surroundings. She lay in bed for a long time, wondering if each of those dials and knobs represented electric grids, substations and companies all over America, ready to send the country into darkness. It was not a pleasant thought, and she forced herself to put it aside as she began her day.

She had just finished her breakfast when Pruden telephoned to ask if she was free for a few minutes, he needed to talk.

"Free until half past nine," she told him.

He must have been calling from his police car because three minutes later she was opening the door to him. "Turkish coffee?" she asked.

He grinned. "You're an exotic influence on me. The first time you offered—"

She laughed. "I remember, yes."

"I felt you were testing me," he told her, "so I said Turkish and nearly strangled from it." He followed her into the kitchen while she measured and prepared it. "I'm here about the carnival that comes every summer and sets up on the outskirts of the suburb of Edgerton. The owner's a reliable chap named Max Saberhagen, runs a clean, honest show. Rides, Ferris wheel, and the usual fortune-teller, a good money-maker, very popular, named Shana."

She handed him the carafe of coffee to carry into the living room, and followed him with two cups. "And?" she asked, as they sat down on opposite couches, facing each other.

"Max is worried; he suspects what he calls 'hanky-panky' going on."

Amused, she said, "I know that word; what's happening?"

He sighed. "In Trafton we have several gangs to keep an eye on. Every big city has them; they come and they go, but one in particular is too damn clever and canny for us, and he's behind most of the major crime in Trafton. Name of Jake Bodley, and—"

Madame Karitska nodded. "I've heard of him."

Pruden gave her a startled glance. "Even you? At any rate Max knows Bodley's people only too well; his carnival's been coming here for seven summers, and in the early years he was approached by Bodley and his men demanding a payoff for protection. Max flatly refused each time. At first they made a little trouble—a flurry of pickpocketing, bad for a carnival's reputation, but Max has steadfastly refused to pay them, and for the past few years they've left him alone."

"But not now?" she asked.

"No. For the past week or ten days Bodley's men have been spotted at the carnival every evening."

"Doing what?" she asked.

"Strolling."

"Just *strolling?*"

"Yes, but with a special interest in the fortune-teller Shana."

"Interesting," said Madame Karitska. "She must be very attractive?"

"We don't think she's the attraction," he told her. "Not for Jake Bodley. His specialty is drugs, and robberies to pay for the drugs, and the carnival's only half a mile away from the throughway to New York; it could be an easy dropoff place for him if he's found his other routes blocked."

"You think he could somehow be using the carnival for deliveries?" she asked.

Pruden shrugged. "If so, we have no idea how. We only know that suddenly his men have been showing a distinct interest in the carnival. That's something new, and Max is worried. *His* fear is that they're looking for a way to put him out of business as revenge for refusing to pay protection money— and heaven only knows they could do a hell of a lot of damage: sabotage the Ferris wheel, or slip a few gears on the merry-go-round."

"But you think different?" asked Madame Karitska.

Pruden nodded. "It's not Bodley's style. If it's revenge he's after—as Max fears—he'd very definitely catch Max in a dark alley and his body would be found floating in the river weeks later. Bodley is *not* subtle. But there's no explaining his men coming to the carnival suddenly, different men each night— and so regularly." He added abruptly, "I'm filling you in with a lot of details."

"Yes, you are," she said dryly. "The chief sent you, didn't he, and this is *not* idle conversation over coffee?"

"True," admitted Pruden. "I had orders to fully brief you first. On the carnival, on Max, on Jake Bodley and his gang appearing at the carnival every night this past week, and on our private suspicions that drugs may be involved, but now," he said angrily, "it's become a police matter. The fortune-teller Shana's disappeared."

"Disappeared!"

He nodded. "Didn't come to work last night. Nobody's seen her, she didn't sleep in her trailer and her clothes are still there, and Max is really alarmed. Seems carnival people are like a family; Shana's been with them for three years."

Madame Karitska nodded. "And you think this could have something to do with the Bodley gang?"

"We look at it this way: if there really are drugs coming in by way of the carnival she could have been involved. Or," he said, "she may have learned too much and been frightened and left. *Or* they approached her this week to make a deal, and they threatened her. *Or,* he added reluctantly, "she could have been kidnapped before she talked, *or*—" He didn't finish. "We suggested to Max that a policewoman take her place, but he wants instead to close her tent until we find her. Which, of course, may be impossible."

Madame Karitska waited. "And you?"

"We want to learn what was going on in the tent while we look for her, and why it was of such interest, why Bodley's men, usually two at a time, take a ride or two, but always—

every time—visit Shana's tent. And although a policewoman was suggested . . ." He shook his head. "Just as we have mug shots of almost everyone in Bodley's gang, I'm sorry to say that he can smell the police, man or woman, a mile away, or how else would he have survived a decade being the kingpin of crime in Trafton? And what would a policewoman know about fortune-telling?"

"I begin to see why you're here," she said dryly.

He nodded. "Yes, you could help us, just until we find Shana. Evenings only, five P.M. to midnight, and Max is prepared to pay you handsomely."

"I see."

"It could be dangerous," he told her. "I won't kid you about that, but your being psychic would be an advantage, and with your instincts you just *could* identify Bodley's men if they continue lurking around the tent—if, of course, Shana only ran away. If she's dead . . ." He winced. "If she's dead, we could only hope they proposition *you*. We'd supply some protection but we can't be obvious."

"Fortune-telling," she mused. "I'd have to fake it, I'm afraid, or use tarot cards. No one would care to hand over a watch, a ring, or a wallet in a carnival."

"You mean you'd do it?" asked Pruden eagerly.

"I've always enjoyed carnivals," she said, "except that in Europe they're usually called fairs. Actually it could be a pleasant change. That poor child, of course I'll do it."

"Good," he said with relief. "You'll find the tent dim. No candles—strict regulations from the fire department—only two low-wattage bulbs—so nobody may notice the change; if they do, just tell them Shana's sick."

She said doubtfully, "In a dim tent I don't know what faces I could see to read their reactions."

"Not *that* dim," he assured her, "and people talk. People ask interesting questions, don't they? One of Bodley's men may even want to learn if their future holds prison bars or pub bars." He frowned. "For one thing, we hear that Bodley's taken on a new man this year, a foreigner, and his name might be mentioned. But what it comes down to—all that we know, *really*—is that Bodley's men arrive, lately, every evening, and you might learn something. And that Shana's disappeared . . . Max has a robe you can wear; have you a turban?"

She nodded. "And dangling gold earrings, of course."

"Perfect. If you can start tonight, Margolies will pick you up fifteen minutes before five, deliver you to Max, Max will show you to the tent and send you home at midnight in a cab." With a nod he rose. "Now I've got to get back to work. Two robberies in two nights, it's keeping us busy. And thanks *very* much."

He left her pondering just what manner of fortunes one told in a carnival; out of necessity they would have to be sketchy and brief, but faces had always interested her, each one of them a map of their personality.

You will have good health. . . . I foresee a possible accident, quite serious, near the end of the year. . . . Someone loves you whom you've taken no notice of . . . you will live a long life.

Glib, but viable.

"And always look at their ring finger," she reminded herself, and before welcoming her half-past-nine client she went to her desk to look for her pair of dangling gold earrings.

Seated beside Margolies in his police car Madame Karitska headed toward the suburbs, past a line of malls, then neat lawns and flower gardens, the houses growing smaller as they passed through the center of Edgerton, and once near its border then met with a baseball field on their left, a brilliant green in the sunlight, and to the right of them flags and pennants advertising, quite unnecessarily, MAX'S CARNIVAL OF DELIGHTS, FUN FUN FUN!

Max was waiting for them at the entrance, and once Margolies had introduced them he drove away, leaving Madame Karitska and Max to appraise each other. She liked him: a well-built, sturdy man with a round face that under different circumstances she guessed would be cheerful, but today he looked grim. After *his* close scrutiny he nodded. "You'll do. Good . . . and thanks."

As he led her through the gate into the carnival she smiled at the familiar smells of buttered popcorn and sawdust, the sound of barkers shouting, the merry-go-round pumping out its music, and the undercurrent of grinding machinery and shuffling of feet along the midway. Nodding at the tent as they approached it Max said, "Shana put in long hours—we all do. Then we take a vacation after we close up here, and later head south to set up in Florida for the winter. Shana's been with us three years; she doesn't deserve this."

"No one does," she said quietly.

The tent was striking: it was black with blazing white stars and crescent moons woven into its fabric. Reaching into the interior Max brought out the sign FORTUNES TOLD! SHANA! LEARN YOUR FUTURE, $3.50, and hanging it up over the entry he said, "You're in business now."

Inside, in the center of the room, stood a table draped in bright red satin, a crystal ball displayed prominently on it. Max switched on two feeble lights, one in each corner, and said, "The police had an electrician here today; you'll find"—he bent under the table and pointed—"a buzzer connected to Andy's cotton-candy booth next to you. If you run into any trouble—the police insisted on this—you press it with your foot. Better look where it is now so you don't accidentally step on it."

She leaned over, and then because the drapery cut off all light she knelt and ran her hand over the earth until she found a tiny metal bubble in the corner.

"Tryout time," said Max, and went out and alerted her cotton-candy neighbor Andy. Once back he said, "Okay, press the buzzer."

Madame Karitska, still kneeling, did as she was ordered and heard a distant voice shout, "Okay, Max—okay!"

"Very clever," she acknowledged.

With a nod he said, "There'll be customers for you soon—good luck." And he strode away, leaving her in a dim tent in which its original occupant had either fled for some unknown reason, or had been kidnapped or murdered. Not a pleasant thought, but bringing out her tarot cards—just in case—she saw that her first customer had arrived, an eager

young girl in blue jeans with a knapsack at her back. Her job
had begun.

Although the tent was dim the crystal ball picked up what
light there was and added sparkle. And people came . . . a
whole strata of people came, and she felt at first overwhelmed, accustomed as she was to five or seven clients a day,
and discussions in depth; overwhelmed, too, by questions she
could scarcely answer without psychometry. The young
women and the teenage girls wanted to know if love, a career,
a marriage awaited them; the men—but there were few of
them—whether a better job could be had, or if their wives
were really faithful. Knowing a little of palmistry she began to
read palms, and if she found a disturbing lifeline it was easier,
given a distinct clue. . . . "You must be more careful of your
health; there could be an accident or illness waiting for you
in"—frowning—"six or seven years if you do not cut down on
stress."

At the end of the evening, at midnight, she drew a deep
sigh of relief, and hung Shana's blue robe on a hook. In the
space of seven hours she must have seen over twenty-five
people; she had learned how fashionable knapsacks had become, whether leather purses slung over the backs of virtual
dowagers, or canvas knapsacks worn by the young—it was not
a style that had reached Eighth Street yet—and she had
learned how many troubled and confused people there were
in the world, but she had learned nothing that could help
Max or the police.

Max had summoned a cab for her; she handed him the bag

containing the profits from her evening and said, "Any news yet?"

He shook his head. "Not a word."

The next day was less pressured; calls for an appointment that day she moved ahead a week, and there were only two clients whom she'd been unable to cancel, not knowing how to reach them. She was able to rest, meditate and clear her mind for the work that lay ahead. Pruden called once, to report no progress on finding Shana; he himself was still busy investigating yesterday's robberies but he hoped she was having that pleasant change that she'd mentioned.

She admitted only to its being a change, and did not mention that it had proven unexpectedly demanding after a day with clients of her own.

On the second night, however, she reached the carnival feeling far more prepared and relaxed. The sun was bright, the air was crisp and cool, and arriving a few minutes early, and seeing the merry-go-round halted, she bought a ticket and experienced an exhilarating ride on a black horse that galloped slowly up and down to the beat of "In The Good Old Summertime." Thoroughly refreshed, she walked to Shana's tent and hung the sign over its entrance. It was five o'clock, and she was ready for business.

After a short wait a young woman peered into the tent, and once assured that it was occupied she entered with a knapsack that she deposited just inside the entrance. "Heavy," she explained as she sat down across from Madame Karitska to ask if there was a better job in her future. "All I do is file things," she complained, "but in high school I got A's in shorthand and business."

Madame Karitska studied the girl's face and then the crystal ball, and at last told her that yes, she could feel her discontent, but within the space of two years she would experience a happy change in her life, but she must be careful about the men in her life until then. Feeling like an utter hypocrite she had to remind herself that she was doing this for Shana as she struggled to find more to say.

When the girl left, Madame Karitska saw that she'd forgotten the knapsack that she'd left at the entrance, and this prompted Madame Karitska to think wryly that if she was this absentminded she'd do well to remain in her existing job.

Two customers later a young man thanked her for her advice and as he left he picked up the girl's knapsack and vanished. She would have run after him and rescued it for the girl but her next customer was already seating herself, a woman whose anxiety seemed to fill the tent as she poured out a story of a husband who beat her, and with tears in her eyes asked if she should leave him when she had no money. In this case, thanks to Jan at the Settlement House, Madame Karitska was able to give her the names and addresses of two safe houses for shelter once she felt strong enough to leave.

There was next a fidgety and very nervous young man in hiking boots, with a knapsack that he dropped at the entrance. Once seated he explained that he'd been offered a guide's job at a state park but he was afraid he'd lose his girlfriend if he should take it. Studying her crystal ball she assured him the experience would be good for him, and a bright future lay ahead, and he left, looking gratified, but leaving his knapsack behind him. Again her first instinct was to call after him, because in spite of the dim light his knapsack remained clearly *there*.

A curious coincidence, she thought, suddenly alert, and determined to keep an eye on this second knapsack so absentmindedly left behind.

Two customers later a stout man in his fifties sat down to quiz her about his wife's faithfulness, and after she'd managed a few predictions, and the suggestion that he send his wife flowers and pay more attention, he nodded politely, rose, and as he left he picked up the knapsack that had been left by the nervous young man in hiking boots. Again she resisted that first instinct to call to him that it was not his knapsack, but another man had already entered, surprisingly well dressed for a carnival in suit and tie, and a vest as well. He was also carrying a small suitcase that he put down beside the entrance, and she eyed this with interest before transferring her attention to this man. He said he *knew* it was nonsense, this fortune-telling, but he was a traveling salesman and did she see in his future a better job than the one where he felt overworked and underpaid.

"I do, yes," she told him, and after adding reassurances and a few encouraging predictions she waited to see if he carried his small suitcase out with him, but in leaving he ignored his small suitcase and vanished.

This was one too many coincidences for Madame Karitska

and this time she rose, left her chair, and brought the suitcase to place out of sight under the table that was so heavily draped in silk satin that it reached the floor.

An hour later a woman with brassy blond hair and a heavily made-up face arrived, wearing a red-flowered knapsack that she left just inside the entrance before seating herself opposite Madame Karitska. She gave her a shrewd but not unkind appraisal. "You're not Shana," she told her. "She promised me a real flashy guy loaded with cash."

"How long ago was that?" asked Madame Karitska pleasantly.

She shrugged. "Last week. And he ain't shown up yet."

Madame Karitska smiled and said, "Ah, but patience is needed; dates are always difficult in the psychic world."

After Madame Karitska's few remaining words on the psychic world, and much staring into the crystal ball, the woman rose, left a tip on the table and walked out, leaving the bright red-flowered knapsack behind her, at the entrance.

Again Madame Karitska walked to the entrance and brought the red knapsack back to shelter under her table, next to the suitcase. The evening, she thought, had begun to be very, very interesting, and she wondered just who would arrive to retrieve the flowered knapsack, or to leave something else behind.

It was an hour before closing time when a rough-looking man entered the tent and stopped at the entrance, looking puzzled. "Hey," he called to her, "my wife left a suitcase here. I've come for it. Small brown one."

If he had asked for the brassy blond woman's red-flowered

knapsack the suspicions she harbored might have dimin-
ished; she might even have given it to him. But no wife had
left the suitcase; it had been left behind by the man who had
described himself as a traveling salesman and who inquired
about his future. Definitely it had been his. She said in a mild
voice, "It doesn't seem to be there."

"You never seen it? A small brown suitcase?"

"It's been a busy evening," she told him, and with her left
foot she felt for the buzzer under the table and pressed it.

He gave her a hard glance and withdrew, but she could
hear him talking angrily and loudly to someone just outside
the tent. She hoped the next man to enter would be Max
or possibly Margolies, but it was instead a stranger, a very
confident-looking man in a suit and tie, with a smile that did
not reach his cold blue eyes that flicked over her dismissively,
as if she were a mere object.

He was followed by the man who had just left. "This the
woman, Ben?"

Ben said eagerly, "That's her, boss."

His boss said in a dangerously calm voice, "So where's the
suitcase? You kept it for yourself, maybe? Stole it from Ben?"

"On the contrary," she told him coldly. "He mistakenly insisted that his wife left it, but it was definitely left by a man."

"Then you have it here," he said, and left the entrance to
walk toward her. "Where is it? Under that table?"

It suddenly occurred to her that her neighbor Andy could
have been too busy to hear the buzzer, and that she was going
to be forced to give this man the suitcase. But there was still

the knapsack, which didn't appear to concern him, and she said quickly, to prevent his seeing the knapsack, "I'll get it for you." Moving the chair away from the table she knelt down, lifted the satin drape, pushed the knapsack farther to the rear, pressed the buzzer a second time, urgently, and dragged out the suitcase, at which point he gave her ankle a savage kick. Unable to stand up, her ankle throbbing, she had to watch him take possession of the suitcase.

"It isn't yours," she told him angrily. "It's you who's stealing now."

"One more insult, lady," he said, "and I'll give you a hell of a slap."

"I wouldn't do that, Bodley," said a wonderfully familiar voice, and stumbling to her feet Madame Karitska gasped, "Pruden—thank God!"

The man called Bodley pulled an efficient-looking pistol out of his pocket and pointed it at Pruden. "I've never liked you, Lieutenant, and I'd really love to pull the trigger and shoot—and nobody'd hear it with all the noise outside."

Madame Karitska sighed. She abhorred violence, but obviously this was a time to put aside her scruples; she reached for the crystal ball, and since Bodley's back was turned to her she took several steps toward him, lifted the crystal ball, and shattered it over his head. He fell to the floor, leaving Ben to make small whimpering sounds of protest at seeing his boss unconscious.

Pruden said incredulously, "Neat work! My God, you saved my *life*!" To Margolies, who had just caught up with him and was entering the tent, he said, "She knocked him out, bless her. Can you believe it? Watch Bodley will you?" and as Max followed Margolies into the tent he turned to Madame Karitska. "What was going on here? What brought Bodley here?"

She said unsteadily, "I think I've found how they do it. This tent has to be a dropoff for *something* . . . knapsacks left at the door, picked up later by someone else, a sort of relay system to throw you all off the trail. Mr. Bodley was after this suitcase. There's a knapsack, too. You really think you'll find drugs?"

"I don't expect Barbie dolls," growled Pruden, and then, "Damn, this suitcase is locked. You say there's a knapsack, too?"

She returned to the table and drew out the knapsack. Pruden, keeping an eye on Ben, unzipped it and brought out one of many neatly wrapped white packages, and with his penknife slit a hole from which he drew out a handful of white powder. "Heroin," he said. "Top quality, too. The best. Margolies, handcuff Bodley before he regains consiousness."

"His feet are moving," pointed out Madame Karitska, with a nod to Bodley.

"Thanks. You have something to gag him with, Margolies, so he won't tell us what good lawyers he has, and how this is police harassment?"

Margolies brought out a handkerchief and stuffed it into Bodley's mouth. "Sorry, Jake," he said as a startled Bodley opened his eyes." You'll have to breathe through your nose now." And to Pruden, "So what's in the suitcase? You broke the lock?"

"I think we've got cocaine here. Between the two of these

I'd guess we're looking at a million dollars' worth of the stuff." To Max he said, "Clever, weren't they?"

Max shuddered. "Clever enough to have ruined me."

Bodley, inert but conscious, made strangled noises of protest. Looking down at him Pruden said, "You realize, Bodley, the minute you claimed the suitcase and knapsack, and with three witnesses, you've been caught at last . . . ? *Very* conclusive evidence, but it would go a hell of a lot easier for you if you tell us now what you know about Shana's disappearance," and removing the handkerchief stuffed in the man's mouth, "We'd like to hear about that."

"You can all go to hell," Bodley told him furiously.

"Oh, I doubt that, I doubt that," said Pruden. "Book him, Margolies."

Together Margolies and Ben pulled a groggy Bodley to his feet, and one on each side of him, they escorted him out of the tent.

Pruden's interest in Bodley faded as he looked at Madame Karitska and then at Max. "I'm sorry, Max, it was at best a feeble hope, I'm afraid we've learned nothing about Shana."

"You haven't, no," said Max accusingly. "Couldn't you have forced him to tell you?"

Pruden sighed. "After it really hits him that he's going to jail—a new experience for him—he just might talk, but it would be too late for Shana, and I doubt he'd do it. Bodley's tough."

"And there's *nothing* you can do for Shana, nothing at all?" demanded Max. "Naturally I'm grateful they'll no longer use my carnival for smuggling, but what's important to me—to the carnival—is to find Shana."

Madame Karitska considered the lateness of the hour, her throbbing ankle, and then Shana. "I might be able to help," she told them.

The two men turned to stare at her. Pruden said, "But . . . with *psychometry?*"

She smiled at him forgivingly. "You're forgetting how Jan was located, once we knew that she was alive and somewhere out in Trafton, but with no idea *where.*"

"But Jan happened to be psychic," he protested, "and you and young Gavin and Faber-Jones, the three of you psychic-projected—"

She interrupted him to say, "There are other methods, Pruden, and it's worth a try."

"You mean," said Max, "there's still hope? Do you actually mean there's something you can *do?*"

She nodded, and to Pruden, "I would need a very large and very detailed map of Trafton, a quiet room somewhere, and a photograph of Shana. No promises, but possible."

"You'll have it," agreed Pruden. "We've a conference room on the top floor at headquarters, and of course we've a large and detailed map of the city." He glanced at his watch, and then at Madame Karitska. "Nearly midnight, you're not too tired?"

"To help find a victim of that dreadful man? Of course not."

Max said, "But it's dark, it's night."

"It will be light in six hours," she pointed out.

"So let's go. Anything else you need?"

"Yes, six or eight inches of string, as thin as possible, and above all a photograph of Shana, please."

It needed only a few minutes until Max returned to them with a publicity portrait of Shana, as well as string. They walked out of the tent and again into the world of calliope music, of shouts from the ring tossers and screams from the Ferris wheel, to leave the carnival behind and enter Pruden's police car.

This time he turned on the siren to cut a way for them through the night traffic, and once at headquarters they were whisked up in the elevator to the top floor.

"This is the conference room," Pruden said, opening a door and turning on lights. There were chairs lining the long mahogany table and Pruden pushed six or seven to one side. In the huge windows they were reflected like pale ghosts against the darkness outside, while below them the neon signs of nightclubs, traffic lights and cars glittered like up-side-down stars. The map was carefully spread out on the table. Madame Karitska removed one of her long gold earrings and attached it to the string.

Max said suddenly, "But that looks like dowsing! I grew up in Vermont, where every town seemed to have a chap who could locate water for a well by dowsing."

Madame Karitska gave him an appreciative glance. "But we will be dowsing for a human being. Lower the lights, will you, Pruden?" and she gave the photograph of Shana a long look: a heart-shaped young face, long blond hair, and bright blue eyes.

"She's not psychic," Max said abruptly, "but she's warm and caring and good with people."

"I can see that," said Madame Karitska. "Now we must be very quiet."

They watched as she closed her eyes for a few minutes, and then, opening them, she leaned over the map, lightly holding the earring suspended on its string. It swayed nervously and then steadied itself, and for long moments Pruden feared defeat until the earring began to tremble and started to move, hovering briefly over the center of the city and then slowly, very slowly, with Madame Karitska's hand obeying, it came to a stop.

And there it remained still.

"Where has it stopped?" asked Madame Karitska.

"Railroad Avenue. Not the best section of town. Freight depot, billiard parlors, repair shops, truck depot, garages."

"I have the impression . . ." began Madame Karitska.

"Yes?" said Max eagerly.

She frowned. "The impression that she's somewhere in a box."

"A box!" blurted out Max. "Dead or alive?"

"I don't know; it's blurred. *Not* a coffin. A box or crate."

"She can't be alive," Max said despairingly. "We'll never find her."

Pruden paid him no attention. "As soon as it's light we'll try Railroad Avenue. I'll clear it with the chief. Knowing we've finally caught Jake Bodley he should be in a *very* good mood, practically ecstatic."

"Five hours' sleep will help," said Madame Karitska. "You'll pick me up, please, at six o'clock?"

"I insist on going, too," Max said firmly. "You'll find me downstairs here in your lobby at five-thirty A.M."

Dropping string and earrings into her purse she smiled at him. "You're not married, Mr. Saberhagen?"

He shook his head.

"Does Shana know you're in love with her? Have you told her?"

With an attempt at humor he said, "Deliver me from psychics! Of course she doesn't know, I'm too old for her, I know that, and she'd never—But oh God I hope she's still alive."

There was no reply, no reassurance that he could be given. Madame Karitska was delivered back to her apartment, where she applied a cold compress to her savagely kicked ankle, brewed a cup of valerian tea, printed a sign, CALLED AWAY ON EMERGENCY, to hang on her door in the morning, and went to bed.

Railroad Avenue was three miles long, and starting at the north end it grew more derelict as it left behind the more prospering businesses. Pruden named each building as they passed, but these grew thinner as they approached Roosevelt Boulevard.

"Not much at this end," he said. "On your right a liquor store—cheap liquor—and two boarded-up shops. On your left there used to be a park; now it's called Shanty Town—or

Little Paris, its occupants have named it. The city plans to clear it out soon and build a mall." He waved a hand vaguely toward it. "Rather tough on the homeless, and with unemployment so high it's grown like weeds. Quite a fire hazard, too, those shelters built out of wooden discards and plastic and—"

Madame Karitska said abruptly, "And boxes and crates? Stop, Pruden, stop!"

He braked sharply. "Boxes and crates," he repeated. "*Yes,*" and he drove to the edge of the weed-rimmed street and parked the car. "They don't like policemen in there," he said grimly as he opened the door to Madame Karitska and Max, "but let's look."

There was certainly no formal entrance to Little Paris; they entered between two shacks built out of cheap plywood. Ahead of them a woman sat in the sun nursing a baby; seeing them she scuttled into the tent behind her. It was like a labyrinth, with its variety of makeshift housing, and after considerable wandering Madame Karitska suspected they were lost until she saw ahead of them a propped-up door being removed by mysterious hands and set aside to allow a man to emerge from his shack into the sunshine. He stood by the door, looking them over, as if waiting: fortyish, thinning red hair and wearing patched jeans and a stubble of beard.

As they neared him he appeared to have reached a decision. He said, "You looking for a pretty little blond lady that got tossed out of a car three nights ago?"

"Tossed out of a— Yes, *sir,*" gasped Max. "You've seen her?"

Again he looked them over carefully. "Bert and I been looking after her," he said. "Didn't know her name, and no purse
to ID her. She was hurt pretty bad; that car must have been
going fifty miles an hour."

Pruden said, "We've been looking for her, yes. She's inside?"

"And may we come in?" asked Madame Karitska politely.

He smiled. "She'll be glad to see *you*," he told Pruden, his
eyes running over his police uniform. "If the liquor store's
phone hadn't been out of order we'd have called nine-one-
one. They damn near killed her, Bert and I saw it."

But Max had already rushed past him to disappear inside
the shack, and they followed him out of the sun into a dim interior. "She's alive," he shouted.

Shana lay on a ragged mattress, her blond hair stiff with
blood, one cheek swollen, her eyes bruised, and as she looked
at Max her eyes were filled with wonder. "You found me, Max.
Oh, you *found* me!"

Their hosts' companion, obviously the buddy he'd called
Bert, was kneeling over a Sterno stove and stirring soup in a
pan. Glancing up he said, "Take care, we think her left arm's
broken, too."

Sternly Pruden said, "Bodley did this?"

"I don't know *who* he was, but you won't arrest Bert and Al,
will you? They've been so kind—so very kind. They built a fire
outside and heated water to wash the gravel out of the cuts
on my face, and . . . yes, even stole two cans of tomato soup
for me—I'm sorry, Bert, but I heard you did—and you won't
arrest them, will you?"

"Arrest them?" echoed Max, turning to look at Bert. "I

can't give them medals but I can give them jobs if they'd care to work in a carnival."

Bert abandoned the soup to look up at him. "You hear that, Al? A *job?*"

"I heard," he said, and a huge grin spread across his face. Pruden said stubbornly, "Yes, but was it a man named Bodley?"

She turned her bruised face toward him. "He didn't tell me his name. I was such a fool; I told him I'd call the police and . . . and he knocked me around and forced me to go with him to the car. And he drove it."

Al said, "Bert and I can ID the man, we were out looking for cigarette butts when it happened. He just opened the door and pushed her out. We got a good look at him, too."

"Well, well," said Pruden, looking pleased. "Looks as if we'll have Bodley for attempted murder as well as narcotics. I'll call an ambulance now from my car. Back in a minute."

Max was kneeling beside Shana and smoothing her hair. Madame Karitska, feeling that the situation was well under control without her, enjoyed observing the ingenuity applied to the twelve-by-twelve shack. It amused her to wonder the reactions that she'd produce if they knew that as refugees her family had lived in just such a makeshift hut in Kabul: boxes for tables, large tin cans overturned to sit on, a kerosene lamp.

Pruden, returning, said, "Ambulance on its way."

Madame Karitska glanced at her watch. "It's only half past eight," she told him. "If you could take me home now I believe I can remove the sign on my door and still see my nine o'clock client."

"Okay with me. You'll stay, Max?" he asked.

"Of course," he said.

Madame Karitska turned to leave and then looked back at Max, still hovering over Shana. "By the way," she said in a kind voice, "I do believe, Mr. Saberhagen, that if you share with Shana what you admitted to us last night I think the results could surprise you."

On that note—she had always enjoyed a good exit line— she left to accompany Pruden to his car.

16

Several days later, fully restored from her encounter with the infamous Jake Bodley, Madame Karitska climbed the stairs to pay her monthly rent and to see what new snakes Kristan might have devised for his painting.

A surprise awaited her: as Kristan opened the door to her, his smock as usual splattered with paint, she looked beyond him at his easel and exclaimed, "Kristan!"

His grin was almost boyish. "Like it?"

The painting on his easel was an abstract tangle of brilliant colors—pink, orange, red, yellow, purple—the shapes so intertwined that it needed a second glance to realize the sinuous forms that filled the canvas were snakes.

"They almost move," she said in awe, walking past him to look more closely. "And what *color!*" and with an interested glance at him, "Very different from your dark, Rousseau-like designs."

"So something finally pleases you," he said dryly as she handed him her rent money, and he added, "I never thought—"

He was interrupted by a woman's voice from the kitchen, calling, "Is an egg sandwich okay, Kristan?"

There was something very familiar about that voice, and she looked at Kristan with curiosity.

"Egg's fine," he called back.

"Good," was the reply, "because—" and Betsy Oliver walked out of the kitchen carrying a plate that she almost dropped at seeing Madame Karitska. "Oh how wonderful," she said. "I didn't know you were here. I'm so glad to see you again!"

"And I you," said Madame Karitska, smiling. "I see that you two artists are—"

"—are thinking of living together," Kristan told her. "You might as well be the first to know, since you live downstairs."

Betsy nodded happily. "We'll be neighbors. His apartment is larger than yours, you see. There's a bedroom for Alice, and we think my drawing table will fit"—she gestured toward a corner of the room—"over there by the window."

It was not often that Madame Karitska found herself without words, but firmly dismissing her astonishment she said, "I'm delighted; we really will be neighbors. And how *is* your artwork going?"

"Tell her," said Kristan.

"Gladly," and turning to Madame Karitska, "Kristan's been such a help. I draw figures now, too, and a publisher who saw my greeting-card drawings has asked me to illustrate a children's book."

"A rather *gushy* book," put in Kristan.

"Oh, Kristan, not *gushy*," she told him, and to Madame Karitska, with a humor that she'd never shown before, "It has no snakes, you see, just a cuddly brown bear and children. Alice posed for it."

Remembering the events of two days ago, Madame Karitska felt almost uncomfortable at the happiness flooding the room. She knew Kristan only as a responsible young landlord with little conversation. That he had opened his life not only to Betsy but to her five-year-old daughter suggested hidden depths and a Kristan that she'd never met, for it was a rare man, she thought, whose caring could include Alice as well as Betsy, and she would look forward to knowing him better.

"I'm really glad for you," she told them, "but I'll leave you now to your egg sandwiches because I have two appointments ahead of me and three guests coming to dinner tonight."

But Betsy followed her out to the stairs. "I wanted to say . . . I think of it so often now," she said with a smile. "It's just like what you told me that day. Your philosophy, I guess you'd call it. It left me that time with a feeling of *patterns*, somehow, especially when I think how it was you who introduced me to Kristan, and just see what's happened now!"

Madame Karitska nodded. "You love him."

"Yes, and it's so different. With Alpha—I mean Arthur—I realize now he'd never really grown up, even though he treated me like a child. With Kristan . . . well, we're equals, he actually *respects* me."

Madame Karitska leaned over and kissed her on the cheek. "Meaningful coincidences again," she murmured, remembering Roger Gillespie, and giving Betsy a hug she descended the stairs to her own apartment in time to see the postman sorting mail on the steps.

Opening the door she said, "Good morning, Mr. Petrie, anything but bills for me today?"

He was a likable young man. He grinned and said, "Surprise . . . a letter and also a postcard sent Priority Mail." He shook his head. "Never saw a postcard sent by Priority Mail, and"—turning it over—"a mighty queer one, too." He handed her the two missives and moved to Kristan's box and she went inside, closing the door behind her and glancing at the postcard he'd called a mighty strange one.

And strange it was: it had been accurately addressed to her but when she turned it over it was absolutely blank, without message or signature. She was about to toss it into the wastebasket when she saw its postmark: Denby, Maine.

The postmark itself was a message; Roger Gillespie had found what he was looking for, and he wanted her to know. It was kind of him, but remembering the vivid dream she'd had of what he might face she couldn't help shivering. She placed it on her desk and opened the letter to find a check for one thousand dollars from Max Saberhagen.

"One thousand dollars!" she exclaimed aloud—and for only two nights' work? Generous indeed! This, too, she placed on her desk, but the thought of the mysterious postcard lingered, because it meant, surely, that Gillespie had found the source of the destruction that he'd feared. It held an almost biblical quality, this confrontation of good with evil, of life versus death and destruction. The words sent her to her bookcase, where she fingered the Koran, passed lightly over the several books on Buddhism, found the Bible, and opened it to the passage that already haunted her: *And I beheld a pale horse and his name was Death, and Hell followed him. And power was given unto them to kill with sword, and with hunger and with Death.*

If Roger Gillespie failed . . .

He had found Denby but what else had he found, and why had he sent a postcard by Priority Mail, and what did it mean? But there was no one—*no one* she could share this with, because no one else knew of Roger Gillespie's surprising and very private visit to her that day.

But her first client of the day was knocking on the door, and she firmly put aside her speculations, curiosity and dread. Instead she forced herself for the rest of the day to think of the wonderfully generous check sent to her by Max Saberhagen.

For this Friday evening she had invited Faber-Jones, Pruden and Jan for dinner. It was necessary for her dinner parties to be small in number since she could seat only four at the table next to the window, but the food she served more than made up for the deficiencies in space. Tonight she had made an egg-and-cucumber mousse; Faber-Jones had brought a bottle of vintage wine, and Jan and Pruden had contributed a quart of ice cream. The streetlight outside her window delivered a soft glow that reinforced the candle occupying the center of the table. "Always the romantic," commented Jan. "I love candlelight, too."

Over dessert and coffee they talked of recent events: of Shana's progress in the hospital, of Jan's work at the Settlement House, and Faber-Jones of how his daughter Laurie had changed.

"Not only talking to me," he said proudly, "but I mean really, *really* talking, and no more hostility."

"Speaking of hostility," put in Pruden, "I met someone I think we all know, and I have to say that he was not only hostile, but *aggressively* hostile."

"That's hard to imagine," said Faber-Jones. "Who was it?"

"Amos Herzog."

"Hostile?" said Jan. "Why in the world would he be hostile to *you*?"

Pruden turned to Madame Karitska with a smile. "He accused me of keeping you so busy that you've said *no* to marrying him."

This met with a sudden silence until Madame Karitska ended it by saying lightly, "How indiscreet of him. He must have been really peeved if he dared to be hostile to a *police* lieutenant."

Jan said, "Marina, he asked you to marry him, and you turned him down?" Flustered, she added, "I mean, I know he's a lot older than you are, and a retired safecracker, but such a *catch*—all that charm and money!"

Madame Karitska smiled. "Shocking, isn't it? But can you imagine me living on Cavendish Square, or Amos here? We have agreed to remain friends, for I like him very much, but marriage, no."

As she said this the streetlight outside her window flickered and then died, leaving them with only the candle as light. She rose and went to her desk to switch on her desk lamp, except—"It must need a new lightbulb; nothing happens," she told them.

Faber-Jones had gone to the window and opened it to look both to the left and to the right. "Not your lightbulb," he told her. "The entire street's gone dark. Spooky," he added. "Not even a light seen in a window, either."

"Strange," said Pruden, frowning.

"The electric company ought to be told about this," said Faber-Jones indignantly. "If I can use your phone?" He dialed its number and after a minute or two replaced the receiver. In the dim light of the candle he looked puzzled. "I'm not getting through to the electric company. Nothing rings; there's not even one of those obnoxious voices to tell me all the lines are busy."

Pruden said to Madame Karitska, "You mentioned you have a pocket radio. It runs on batteries?"

She nodded and brought it to him from her desk. Pruden, turning it on, was met with only a few crackling sounds and then silence. He said, "I left my cell phone in my car; *that* should work. Satellites and all that."

Jan said suddenly, "I'm getting goose bumps."

Faber-Jones gave her a sympathetic glance. "You really mustn't be nervous. You can't be thinking . . . Almost every winter this happens."

"But it's not winter," pointed out Jan. "There's no storm. There's no wind, either."

"Overload," Faber-Jones said firmly.

Madame Karitska said nothing. They sat and waited, silent and uneasy until Pruden returned from his car. "I got through to police headquarters—partially at least," he told them. "The lights are out all over Trafton, I learned that much before Margolies's voice faded into silence."

Madame Karitska said, "If the lights are out all over the city . . ." She couldn't finish, it would have to mean that Roger Gillespie had failed.

"I'll have to go," said Pruden. "The traffic lights, the phones, the airport . . ." His voice turned harsh. "Got to go before . . . before . . ." And he was gone.

Jan said in an unsteady voice, "He means before the robberies start, and—oh, think of the people trapped in elevators! Is it possible—can it *be* possible—do you remember what Roger Gillespie said?"

So they are all remembering him, thought Madame Karitska, *and so am I, except that I know more than they do, and this surely has something to do with him.*

"Someone ought to call New York—or Trenton," pleaded Jan. "To see if *their* lights are still on." But no one bothered to remind her the phones weren't working.

As lightly as possible, Madame Karitska said, "We still have candlelight, and I've a pack of playing cards somewhere."

But no one responded, and then, abruptly, the street lamp outside her window flickered and burst into light that again streamed through her window, and Madame Karitska closed her eyes and said, "Thank you, God."

With a sigh of relief Faber-Jones said shakily, "It was just a coincidence, had to be. A coincidence, surely."

Jan said with a nervous laugh, "And to think we were all trying not to believe—no, to remember, to think of . . . But you
see? It couldn't have had anything to do with what Roger
Gillespie talked about."

"No," agreed Faber-Jones, "but I have to admit it gave me a
very strange feeling, an entire city blacked out. Your radio
should be operative again, Marina. Turn it on and see if the
local station explains the blackout."

She reached for her pocket radio and obligingly turned to
the local news station in time to hear, ". . . no explanation as
yet for the city and suburbs of Trafton losing their power
but—" He was cut off as a new voice came on to say, "We interrupt this program to report a mysterious explosion in the
town of Denby, Maine within the last half hour, an explosion
that rocked that town of fifteen thousand and was felt as far
south as Bar Harbor. Denby police report that it has been
traced to the old Thomas Jefferson High School abandoned
in 1990 and sold four years ago to an electronic company. It
is not known if it was occupied at the time of the explosion,
or what caused it. . . . We return you now to your regular
station."

Jan said with a sigh, "That's all very well, but it doesn't explain *Trafton's* blackout."

Madame Karitsky wanted to say *Oh, yes, it does, it means
they reached the building just in time, and you don't realize
how lucky we are.*

Because Roger Gillespie had just proved the impossible
had become the possible. And it was not a pleasant thought.

Yet tomorrow life would go on, electric stoves would be

lighted, refrigerator doors opened, computers and televisions turned on, planes would land and cars would fill their gas tanks, the radio and CNN would give more details of the powerful and mysterious explosion in Denby, Maine—if anyone was interested. In the morning she would deposit Max Saberhagen's check in the bank and there would be two clients in the afternoon, Pruden would be compiling a list of Jake Bodley's crimes, Jan would spend half of the day at the Settlement House, and Faber-Jones would visit his daughter at Daniel's Help Save Tomorrow.

Which was ironic, she thought, that because of Roger Gillespie there was—still—a tomorrow.

Until the next time.